SUGAR, SPICE, AND SPRINKLES

SUGAR, SPICE, AND SPRINKLES

Coco Simon

Simon Spotlight

New York   London   Toronto   Sydney   New Delhi

SIMON SPOTLIGHT
An imprint of Simon & Schuster Children's Publishing Division
1230 Avenue of the Americas, New York, New York 10020
This Simon Spotlight edition February 2020
Copyright © 2020 by Simon & Schuster, Inc.
All rights reserved, including the right of reproduction in whole or in part in any form.
SIMON SPOTLIGHT and colophon are registered trademarks of Simon & Schuster, Inc.
For information about special discounts for bulk purchases, please contact Simon & Schuster Special Sales at 1-866-506-1949 or business@simonandschuster.com.
Text by Caroline Smith Hickey
Cover illustrations by Alisa Coburn
Cover design by Alisa Coburn and Hannah Frece
Interior design by Hannah Frece
The text of this book was set in Bembo Std.
Manufactured in the United States of America 1219 OFF
10 9 8 7 6 5 4 3 2 1
ISBN 978-1-5344-5720-1 (hc)
ISBN 978-1-5344-5719-5 (pbk)
ISBN 978-1-5344-5271-8 (eBook)
Library of Congress Catalog Card Number 2019950341

CHAPTER ONE
SWEET SIERRA

I hurried down the school hallway, balancing a large Tupperware container, my reusable lunch bag, my backpack, and a separate small duffel bag that held notes, sheet music, and a granola bar for my band practice later. When you participated in as many activities as I did, you needed to be prepared. It didn't hurt to bring a few snacks, either.

That day's student council meeting had been pushed back twice because of me and my other commitments, like rehearsals with my amazing band, the Wildflowers; my soccer and softball team practices; and my weekly shifts at Molly's, the best ice cream parlor in town, where I worked with my two best friends every Sunday.

Student council was important to me too, though. I loved being the secretary and taking notes and getting to weigh in and vote on upcoming school events and fund-raisers. I was helping to make my school a more fun and friendlier place. What could be better?

So, to make sure everyone on the council knew how much it meant to me that they'd moved the meeting around (twice), I'd spent some time the day before baking cookies to bring to the meeting. People appreciated cookies, especially after school when they were starving.

I broke into a jog as room 215B came into sight. Then I *whooshed* through the door, and all of my bags and packages banged and slapped against the doorframe and desks as I made my way to the big table by the windows. Let's just say my entrance was loud, even for me.

Everyone turned to see if a herd of elephants was coming, and then made faces like, *Oh, it's not elephants, it's just Sierra*. The four student council members (besides me) were already there, even though it was only 3:13 and the school bell had just rung at 3:10. How had they all gotten there so fast? I had practically

2

run from my locker, and it was only one floor down.

Maybe I needed roller skates.

"Hello, everyone!" I said cheerfully. I plopped the large Tupperware container onto the table and began depositing my other bags into a chair. "Help yourselves!"

"Ooooh, what's in here?" asked Claire Bright, sliding her thumb under the corner of the Tupperware lid. Claire was in eighth grade and was president of the student council. She worked *very* hard on all council business and always wanted everything to be just right. "Wow, Sierra. Really, wow! You made *emoji cookies*?"

She pulled one out and held it up to show everyone. I beamed. What had started out as making plain old sugar cookies (round ones—I didn't even use a cookie cutter because I didn't have time for the dough to chill and set) had become much more interesting when I'd discovered we had a lot of yellow food dye. So I'd whipped up some icing and given all the cookies yellow faces, then had had a blast adding eyes and mouths and different common emoji expressions. Even my identical twin sister, Isa, who basically did the opposite of everything I did and would say she didn't like something just because *I* liked it, had stopped by the kitchen to admire them. She'd even gotten into the spirit of things and decorated a few *Yuck!* faces with tongues sticking out.

"These are *awesome*," said Lee Murphy, our treasurer and resident council grump, biting into a well-chosen frowny face.

Hanna Okoye (sixth-grade rep who recently joined the student council) and Vikram Kapoor (vice president) both nodded in agreement and reached into the Tupperware to grab a few for themselves. I waited until everyone had a cookie before choosing a toothy smiley face for myself.

Everyone was munching and smiling, and I could tell it was going to be a good meeting.

Claire, finishing her third cookie, called the meeting to order. "First order of business—let's all thank Sierra for being so nice and bringing us these awesome cookies! I guess it made this meeting worth the wait."

Everyone clapped, and I gave a silly half bow.

"Really, Sierra—you are just soooo nice," Claire said. "Someone asked me the other day about you, and I said Sierra is a *sweetheart*."

Hanna, who tended to be a bit shy in meetings because she was the only sixth grader, said, "Yeah, you are so sweet, Sierra."

"And a good baker, too," said Lee, polishing off his fourth or fifth cookie. "Sweet Sierra."

I was starting to feel a little self-conscious now, like they were describing a cookie, not me. So I jumped right into reading the minutes from the previous meeting, to change the subject.

"We need to plan Spirit Week," I read from my notes, "which includes making a plan for promo materials and an assembly, and also deciding on the themes for the week."

"I love Spirit Week," said Claire. "It's the best! And since it's my last year here at MLK, I want to make sure we do an awesome job, okay?"

"Of course!" I said. "I love Spirit Week too!"

Hanna and the others quickly agreed, and we started brainstorming ideas. We made a list of how many posters we'd need, who was going to make them, and the basics of what they would look like and say. Then we started discussing our assembly, which had mostly been arranged for us and would include a speaker who was an alumna of the school giving a speech titled "Achieving Success under Stress."

I almost felt like *I* could give that speech, since most of the time I was running from one thing to the next, trying to make it all work and be successful. I giggled to myself, thinking how hard my two best friends, Allie Shear and Tamiko Sato, would laugh if I told them I was going to give that speech. They always teased me about my overly busy schedule, and both of them preferred to live life on the slower, calmer side.

"Why are you laughing, Sierra?" asked Lee. "You don't like the red-and-gold idea?"

"Huh?" I said, not realizing I'd tuned out for a moment. I checked my notes, which I'd been taking very diligently, and saw that Lee had suggested having a Red and Gold Day for one of our spirit dress-up days, in honor of our school colors.

"I wasn't laughing at that!" I replied hastily. "I was just thinking of how great Spirit Week is going to be, and it made me happy, so I guess I . . . just happy-laughed." I smiled and shrugged sheepishly, realizing I sounded a little kooky, but better that than admitting I'd been daydreaming and thinking of something else.

Vikram shook his head. "So happy and sweet! You're like a baby bird, Sierra."

I didn't really see how I was similar to a baby bird, but since he seemed to mean it as a compliment, I said nothing and went back to taking notes.

"Do we have some ideas for the other four days of the week?" I asked. "Other than Red and Gold Day, I mean?"

Everyone started shouting out ideas, and I wrote them down as fast as I could.

- *Crazy Hair Day*
- *Inside Out Day*
- *Pajama Day*
- *Sports Jersey Day*
- *Hawaiian Day*
- *Favorite Decade Day*
- *Heroes vs. Villains Day*
- *Favorite Movie Day*
- *Eighties Day*

We were coming up with so many ideas that I didn't know how we'd choose just five total. There were endless possibilities for Spirit Week, which was

7

why it was fun every year, and why I was glad to be on the student council and able to help make these decisions!

I grabbed a second cookie for myself and kept jotting down notes, until the clock read four fifteen.

"Hey, guys, I'm sorry to do this, but I have to leave a little early—I've got a band practice now and I couldn't push it until later. . . ." I hated feeling guilty when I had to leave one thing to go to another, but with my schedule, it happened fairly often.

"It's okay, Sierra," Claire said. "We understand, and I think we've had a really productive meeting today. But leave these delicious cookies behind, will you?"

I had planned to take the extras for my band, but I couldn't say no when Claire was being so nice about me leaving early. So I just smiled and said, "Of course! Enjoy. And I can't wait for Spirit Week! We're going to have so much fun!"

"Bye, Sierra," said Hanna in her soft voice.

I waved to everyone and set off for my bandmate Reagan's house, feeling lighter without the heavy Tupperware container. I couldn't wait to tell the band some of the ideas we'd come up with for Spirit Week.

Then another idea occurred to me. What about a

Rock 'n' Roll Day? That would be fun and easy to do—just dress like your favorite rock star! Spirit Week was always the best week of the year. And I'd gotten to help plan it *and* go spend time with my band.

"Who says Mondays are terrible?" I asked myself as I hiked down the school driveway and headed in the direction of Reagan's house. "If you ask me, I think they're pretty sweet."

CHAPTER TWO

A BLUE SPRINKLE OF HAPPY

"It's slow in here today," said Tamiko, looking at the clock on the wall of Molly's Ice Cream parlor. "We've only had, like, six customers. Maybe I should post a special on social media. Allie, quick! Come up with something photogenic." She gestured frantically at Allie, as if urging her to put out a fire.

Allie and I exchanged a look. Tamiko was terrific with social media and getting customers in the door. But she could also be a *little* too blunt and bossy sometimes without meaning to. I winked at Allie, and she gave me a knowing smile back.

"Ooo-kay," Allie said slowly. "Well, it's Sunday, so how about something like a Sweet End to the Weekend cone? It could be three or four different scoops, with a piece of candy hidden at the bottom of the cone to find at the end—"

Tamiko clapped her hands together excitedly and said, "Yes! Make it now! I'll post it and we'll get some people in here."

Allie got to work while I grabbed her phone to turn up the music that was playing on the speakers. I looked forward to Sundays every week, because every Sunday I got to scoop ice cream and hang out with my two best friends.

Well, technically, I didn't do very much of the scooping. When the three of us worked together, Allie was the super-scooper, creating beautiful, edible works of art; Tamiko was the marketing maven, often dreaming up delicious, original, *personal* concoctions for customers on the spot; and I was the register runner, because I could do math really fast in my head. I never got flustered if the register jammed or when four different people were shoving money into my hands and waiting for their change.

We were a great team, thanks to years of being such good friends.

Allie made the new cone, and Tamiko posted it online. Not one second later, a customer walked into the shop. It was as if we'd asked a genie for a wish. Tamiko winked at me, and we all scooted into our positions.

The customer was a mom with a young toddler. The woman's hair was piled into a messy bun on top of her head, with stray pieces flying every which way. Her scarf was askew, and her purse gaped open, stuffed with a sippy cup, a plastic baggie of snacks, and what looked like a small blanket. She seemed exhausted. I felt tired just looking at her.

Her toddler was red-faced and kept yanking on her arm. "NO, NO, NO, NO, NO, NO," he was yelling, and he even stamped his foot a few times. "I don't *WANNA*."

"Hello!" Allie said cheerfully. "Welcome to Molly's, where all of our ice creams are homemade right here in the store. What can we get you? We've got a special today—a Sweet End to the Weekend cone, which has a hidden surprise at the bottom."

The woman scanned the containers of ice cream and said, "Um, thanks, but I'll just have a double scoop of Coffee and Doughnuts ice cream for me, and a cup of the Cake Batter for my son. Oh, and do you have a cup of coffee to go with the coffee ice cream?"

"We sure do," I said, and Tamiko scrambled to get it ready for her.

"Black. Hot. Extra strong, please," the woman said. I had a feeling that what this woman really needed was a nap.

Allie got to work on the order, and Tamiko snapped a lid onto the coffee while I rang it all up. Allie handed over the finished cone and cup of ice cream, which were both works of art, as always. She made sure her scoops were perfectly round and full. After all, Molly's was her mother's store, and their family needed it to be as successful as possible.

But as soon as the little boy took his cup of ice cream, he started stamping his feet again and yelling, *"I said I wanted BLUE ICE CREAM!"* He quickly flipped over the cup so that the scoops fell onto the floor.

The mother looked like she was going to lose it. She put her hand to her forehead, closing her eyes and sighing deeply.

Allie, Tamiko, and I exchanged a look. We'd never had a kid dump ice cream onto the floor before. Most kids ate it so fast, there wasn't even time for drips.

"Oh, that's no problem at all," I said brightly.

"Really! Allie will get him a fresh cup of something, uh . . . blue, on the house, and I'll clean up the mess."

"Really?" asked the woman.

"Really," said Allie. And I knew she didn't mind me offering it on the house just this once. She and her mother always wanted every customer to leave happy, and I felt it was my job to make sure that happened.

I hurried to get the mop and clean up the mess as Allie made him a cup of Blueberry Wonder, which was more purple than blue, but it was the closest thing we had. As she was placing the cup on the counter, I reached into the sprinkles bin and pulled out a handful of pale blue sprinkles. I arranged them on top of the scoop in a smiley face and said, "Here's a *blue* sprinkle of happy to go with your *blue* ice cream."

The toddler's face lit up, and so did his mother's. "Thank you," she said. "You are so sweet! We'll definitely come back again."

"Yay!" said Tamiko as they left. "Another happy customer. You really are the nicest, Sierra. I mean, Allie and I are both nice too—don't get me wrong— but you are just *extra* nice."

"So true," said Allie, putting her arm around my

shoulders and giving me a squeeze. "You're the nicest person I know. I'm so glad you're my friend."

"Me too," I said, feeling pleased, but also slightly uncomfortable at all the praise. I'd just done what anyone would have done, right?

To change the subject I said, "I forgot to tell you about my student council meeting the other day. We started coming up with ideas for Spirit Week!"

"YES!" Tamiko jumped up and down a few times. "Spirit Week is my *jam*! I get to make so many great outfits!"

Tamiko loved any excuse to make, create, glue— you name it. Her room and her wardrobe were all completely unique and customized.

"Remember Spirit Week in sixth grade?" asked Allie, sounding wistful. "I was still at MLK, and we had Twin Day, and the three of us decided to go as triplets?" Allie, Tamiko, and I used to all go to the same school—Martin Luther King Middle School— but Allie switched to Vista Green School after her parents got divorced.

"And the best part was that Sierra actually *has* a twin but dressed up with us anyway!" added Tamiko.

I smiled. That had been a great day. "It's not like

Isa would have agreed to dress identically with me anyway," I reminded them. "She'd already started her all-black phase by then."

"True, but you could have dressed like *her*," Allie said.

Tamiko nodded.

I was quiet for a minute, dismayed that I hadn't thought of that. It had never occurred to me that I could have offered to wear Isa's style of clothes, because to me they looked so . . . unhappy.

"You're right," I said. "I guess I could have dressed like Isa."

"Back to this year, though," said Tamiko. "What's the plan for the themes? I want to get my glue gun warmed up and ready to go."

"We're still brainstorming," I told her. "So if you guys have ideas, don't be shy!"

Immediately Allie said, "Well, I'd vote for Favorite Book Characters Day, obviously."

I smiled. It was such an Allie suggestion, because Allie loved to read, and she even had her own column called Get the Scoop in her school's newspaper, where she recommended books and the best flavor of ice cream to enjoy while reading each one.

"Book characters! That's perfect—I'll mention it."

"How about a DIY Day?" Tamiko suggested. "Everyone can decorate their own T-shirt with fabric paints and pens at school."

"Oooh, I love that one too." I grabbed my phone and typed the suggestions into my notes section, to make sure I'd remember them for the next student council meeting. "You're both really brilliant, you know."

"The Sprinkle Sundays sisters never disappoint," Tamiko joked, using the special name we had for ourselves.

"That's for sure," said Allie. "Hey, look! A soccer team is coming in. To your stations, ladies!"

Things got busy then for a while and we didn't have much chance to talk. At the end of our shift, Allie's mom, Mrs. Shear, called us all into the back room (or backstage, as she referred to it) for one of the best parts of our job—taste-testing.

"I've been working on this one for more than two weeks," Mrs. Shear said, giving us each a spoonful of smooth dark brown ice cream. "It's called Chocolate Chili. A little different from my usual flavors, so let me know what you think. And please be honest!"

Allie went first. "Wow, Mom. This is amazing! I've never had ice cream that has, you know, a *kick* to it! It's so neat!"

Tamiko tried it next and agreed. "This is awesome, Mrs. S.! It's very refreshing to mix up something traditionally sweet by adding the hot chili spice."

I went last. After so much praise from my friends, I couldn't wait to taste it. But the second the ice cream hit my tongue, I was confused, and not in a good way. It didn't taste *bad*, it just . . . didn't taste like ice cream. I loved the delicious sweet chocolate, but I didn't like the peppery heat of the chili spice. Wasn't ice cream supposed to be just sweet? Why go and ruin it with spices?

Mrs. Shear was watching me anxiously, as were Tamiko and Allie. They wanted to know what I thought.

"Well?" asked Mrs. Shear. "Tell me the truth, Sierra. I value your opinion."

"It's great!" I said, making sure to sound convincing. "Really good." Mrs. Shear sighed with relief, and Allie beamed. I knew she was proud of her mother for opening this store and coming up with so many unique and interesting homemade flavors.

If Allie and Tamiko liked the Chocolate Chili flavor, then other customers might too. It wasn't like I was some kind of ice cream expert. What did I know? I was the register runner, not the taste buds queen.

And anyway, I didn't want to hurt Mrs. Shear's feelings by telling her it didn't really taste like ice cream to me. That wouldn't be nice at all, and I was always nice.

CHAPTER THREE
TWIN IN THE MIDDLE

Walking in the front door of my house, I smelled something amazing. It had to be my dad's cooking.

I dropped my bags and shoes in one of the few empty spots by the front door and hurried past the piles of clutter in the hallway: magazines, the odd box or two, a coatrack, a basket of shoes. I loved that my family lived comfortably in our clutter. Well, most of us anyway. Isa's room was always as neat as a pin, but the rest of us plopped stuff any old place and it worked just fine.

From the kitchen doorway I saw my dad opening the oven door and pulling out a large roasting pan full of delicious-looking meat.

"Papi?" I said. "Do I smell carne con papas?"

Even though I hadn't enjoyed Mrs. Shear's spicy ice cream, my mouth was already watering for my father's tasty meat-and-potato dish. My parents had been born in Cuba, and my father was a fantastic chef of Cuban food. That was where spice belonged, in my opinion.

"*Sí*, Sierra!" my father replied. "It is. I made it just for you."

The table was already set for four, and my mother was helping to plate the food. My stomach grumbled just looking at all the yummy things my dad had made. He and my mother were both veterinarians and ran a veterinary clinic together, working long hours most days of the week. However, the hospital was closed on Sundays, so my dad liked to make a big family meal and have lots of leftovers for the week. I liked it too.

My mom walked over and kissed me on the head. "Sit down. We're ready."

Isa was already at the table in a black hooded sweatshirt, her head bent as she read a book. Isa loved books as much as Allie did, so you'd think they'd still be friends. But Isa had stopped hanging out with Allie and Tamiko (and me) a year or two before, even though when we were younger, they'd all gotten along fine. Isa still said hi when my friends came over to see me, but she wouldn't join us for a movie, go to the mall together, or even sit and have a snack with us. You'd never think we were sisters, much less twins!

"*Hola*, Isa," I said.

"Hey," she replied, not lifting her eyes.

We all sat down and took turns talking about our day. Sunday dinners were a big deal at our house, since during the week Isa or I might be out somewhere and miss dinner, and one of our parents often stayed late at the vet clinic to see sick patients.

"This is delicious, Papi," I said, digging into my food.

Isa mumbled her agreement. "Even better than usual."

"*Gracias*. How were things at Molly's today, Sierra?"

"Good! Mrs. Shear is thinking of introducing a new ice cream flavor with some spice in it—something really different. I taste-tested it this afternoon—Chocolate Chili."

My mom smiled. "What a great idea! I bet I'd love it."

"Allie and Tamiko both did. I thought it was more confusing than good."

"But you love spice," said my mom.

"I know, but ice cream is a dessert! It's supposed to be sweet. I do love spicy Cuban food, but it's a main course. I think things should be what they're supposed to be."

My dad shook his head. "Sometimes. But it's okay to mix it up now and then. We're not all just one thing, you know. Like I'm a vet, but also a wonderful chef, as you like to tell me."

"I guess so," I mumbled. Inside, though, I disagreed. I liked to know what things were, and I liked them to be consistent.

"Tell us what you have going on this week," my mom said. "I want to make sure we have our schedules laid out and synced up."

"I have a few student council meetings after school. We've started planning for Spirit Week," I told everyone. I went on to explain some of our ideas and the plans we were making. I was hoping Isa would join in the conversation, since it was about her school too, but I could tell by the way her head was bent sharply as she ate that she'd snuck her book beneath the table and was reading it in her lap.

"Allie and Tamiko suggested Favorite Book Characters Day and DIY Day," I said.

My dad laughed and said, "That sounds just like them. But what would *your* choice be?"

"I don't know. I like all of them!" I replied.

"How about Twin Day?" my mom suggested. "That would be perfect for you girls. It was so much fun dressing you two in matching outfits when you were little. The same outfit, but in different colors. You both loved it."

My mom beamed as I glanced nervously over at Isa to see what she thought of the idea.

"Isa?" my dad said. "Pull your nose out of your book, *por favor*. What do you think?"

Isa lifted her head slightly and shrugged, not looking at me. "Sure. They could do a Twin Day. But Sierra would choose to dress up with Tamiko—just like she did last year. The days of Sierra and me looking alike are *looooooong* gone." Then she went back to reading the book in her lap.

My mom and dad both looked at me questioningly. I nodded, letting them know that yes, I had dressed up with Tamiko and Allie on Twin Day the year before.

My mom looked down, clearly disappointed.

I felt awful. At the time, Isa had said she'd rather drop dead than dress up with me. But I knew Isa well enough to know that her words didn't always match her feelings, and I should have been more thoughtful. Her tone just now had made it clear that she was still holding that Twin Day against me.

I felt like a disloyal twin. No matter what was going on with Isa and me, I never, ever wanted to hurt her feelings.

Noticing the awkward silence, Papi tried to smooth things over by passing the food around again. "I'm really looking forward to your soccer game on Thursday," he said to Isa. "The semifinals! We'll all be there to cheer you on."

Oh no. No, no, no, no! I had completely forgotten about Isa's game. She played on a super-competitive all-boys travel team (not the regular seventh-grade girls' team I was on at school), and they'd made it to the regional semifinals. And the game was this week.

"Shoot!" I burst out. "Student council booked another meeting for this Thursday, and I said I would be there."

Isa snorted. "Of course you did. You always have an excuse to miss my games. Thanks a bunch, Sisi."

I bristled. Maybe I'd missed a few of her regular games, but it wasn't like she came to all of mine. And anyway, I wouldn't miss her big game this week—I would never do that!

"I'll be there," I said. "I just need to reschedule the meeting, that's all."

I sounded confident, but in the back of my mind I was already worried about having to ask to move another meeting, so soon after the last one. But I would have to make things work.

"Can I be excused, *por favor?*" Isa asked, standing up and tucking her book into the front pocket of her oversize sweatshirt.

My mom nodded, and Isa stomped off. Her bedroom door shut loudly enough that we knew she was annoyed, but not loudly enough to be a slam, because my parents hated slammed doors.

My parents looked at me, and I could tell they were both disappointed that I hadn't dressed up with Isa for Twin Day the year before, and that I'd forgotten about Isa's game. I knew they relied on me to be the one who was easy to talk to and always smoothed the waters, especially since Isa had become so distant in the previous year.

But I wasn't perfect. And anyway, Tamiko and Allie were my Sprinkle Sundays sisters! My best friends for life. We'd had *fun* dressing up together. And wasn't Spirit Week supposed to be fun?

My dad changed the subject to the vet clinic as we finished dinner, and I offered to do the dishes afterward, since I felt so bad. When I was done, I texted Tamiko:

If we did Twin Day again this year, would you want to dress up together?

She immediately replied: Duh! We're Sprinkle Sundays sisters forever!

I slid the phone back into my skirt pocket and headed upstairs. I had a lot of work to do. First I needed to get the council to agree to move Thursday's meeting, and then I had to make sure we had so many great ideas for this year's Spirit Week that we *definitely* wouldn't be choosing Twin Day.

This identical twin couldn't handle it.

CHAPTER FOUR
RED, GOLD, AND GREEN

On Tuesday, Claire asked everyone on the student council to meet after school so we could go to the craft store and buy supplies for the Spirit Week posters and activities. I was relieved I could make it, since the meeting would be over early enough for me to still get to my Wildflowers practice, and because I'd already asked everyone to reschedule Thursday's meeting so that I could go to Isa's soccer game. I was definitely causing the members some scheduling headaches lately, but I always worked hard on student council projects, so I hoped that made up for it.

Lee and I were in the fabric-paint aisle at Tamiko's favorite store, Mitchell's Crafts & Things, when I remembered that I hadn't told the council yet about her DIY Day idea.

"Hey, guys!" I said loudly. "Come here!"

Claire, Hanna, and Vikram appeared from all different directions. I pointed at the huge selection of fabric paints. "Aren't these great? My friend Tamiko suggested we do a DIY Day where everyone decorates their own T-shirt, and we could use these awesome paints."

"DIY?" said Vikram. "Isn't that for girls?"

"No," I answered, surprised by his response. "It just means 'do it yourself.' It has nothing to do with your gender."

"We don't have the budget to buy everyone in the school T-shirts and fabric paint," said Lee matter-of-factly. "That's a budget-breaker, Sierra."

Lee was a good treasurer because he kept track of our funds to the last penny and never made mistakes. But he could also be a little possessive of the money sometimes, as if he were forgetting that the fund belonged to everyone in the school, and that everyone on the student council got to vote on how to use it.

"I think it would be really fun and unique," I said,

continuing to push the idea, and not just because I didn't want Twin Day. I really thought Tamiko had come up with something creative. "I've never heard of another school doing a theme like this."

Hanna said shyly, "You know, we could have everyone bring in their own T-shirt from home and then just buy the paints for them to decorate the shirts in homeroom."

"It's still too much paint and too much money," replied Lee.

"I think Lee's right," said Claire. "But I do really like the idea, Sierra. Very artistic! Let's keep looking."

We hit the poster board aisle next and selected a bunch of pieces to use for posters, as well as a stack of red markers and gold markers to decorate them. I was still a bit stung by Lee's immediate refusal to consider the DIY idea, but I decided to let it go. Maybe he wasn't a very creative person.

I picked up a beautiful apple-green marker, thinking how nicely it would contrast our red and gold on the posters. It might be good for highlighting certain words, or for shading.

"Isn't this one pretty? Let's get it!" I said.

Claire's expression quickly went from happy to

horrified, as if I'd suggested we buy pet cockroaches for everyone. "*Green?* You want to use *green*? That's Vista Green's school color! You know that, right?"

I was so surprised, I could hardly answer. I suppose I knew in the back of my mind that Vista Green's colors were green and white, but what did it matter? We weren't dressing up for a soccer game in the opposite team's colors. We were talking about making posters that would only be hung at our school.

"I, uh, guess I didn't think about it. Anyway, it's not a big deal, is it?"

"They're a *rival school*, Sierra," Claire said. "Not to mention, the kids who go there are total snobs."

Snobs? Allie had mentioned in the past that the kids at her school could be cliquey, but "total snobs" seemed like an exaggeration.

Lee quickly nodded. "It's true. I know a kid who goes there. He says the girls are all clones and dress exactly alike."

Claire added, "Yeah, *and* they all think they're sooooo great because their school is new. They have brand-new classrooms, new lockers, new everything. They even have amazing cafeteria food. And they brag about it to one another all the time. They think we're pitiful because we go to sad, old MLK with the overflow trailer classrooms and the terrible gluey mac and cheese."

Our mac and cheese *was* terrible. And Allie had said that Vista Green had great food. But what did any of that matter? It didn't mean that all the kids who went there were jerks. Allie was definitely *not* a jerk. And her friend Colin and some of the girls that I'd met were all really nice.

Before I could speak up, Claire continued, "Oh my gosh—you guys. I just got the BEST idea! Let's have an Anti–Vista Green Day during Spirit Week!"

Lee's face immediately lit up. "That's a great idea! We can all dress alike and complain about how our steak and lobster lunches aren't cooked *perfectly*, and how our huge new lockers are just *too big*."

Lee and Claire laughed, and even Vikram joined in. Hanna stayed quiet and inspected the wall of markers.

"You guys are just joking, right?" I asked. I couldn't believe that the kids I was on the student council with, who had always been so nice and easygoing, could be so mean-spirited about another school.

Claire shot me an icy glare. "No, of course we're

not joking. This is a great idea. It would really be good for school spirit."

It would be terrible *for school spirit*, I thought. Hating on another school for silly, made-up reasons? That wasn't what Spirit Week was about. That was just unkind.

"What's wrong, Sierra? You don't like the idea?" asked Vikram.

It was my opportunity to speak up and say what I thought—that Anti–Vista Green Day was a terrible idea. But with four pairs of eyes staring at me, the words stuck in my throat. I didn't like to argue, and I didn't want to be the difficult one. I had already made everyone move yet another meeting, and today I had to leave the craft store and rush right to Reagan's house for band.

I was sweet Sierra, who got along with everyone and never made any trouble. And I didn't want all of them yelling at me or getting angry at me.

"I guess it's an okay idea," I said finally. My stomach felt queasy as I said the words, and I quickly walked over to a bin of sale items and pretended to look through them for things we needed.

I was disappointed in myself. Why couldn't I stand

up to Claire and Lee? Just because they were in eighth grade? Or because I didn't want to make them mad and have them kick me off the student council?

Or was it because I was too wimpy to stand up for myself, period?

All through my rehearsal with the Wildflowers, I thought about what Claire and Lee had said. I didn't bring it up with my band, because I didn't feel right discussing student council gossip in front of them, especially unkind gossip. But by the time I got home, the issue was burning like an ember in my stomach. Was there some sort of rivalry between MLK and Vista Green, and because I didn't know about it, I was overreacting to Claire's suggestion? I almost hoped there was, so that she wouldn't seem as mean and unfeeling as she had at the craft store.

I was in luck when I got home—Isa was at the kitchen counter, making herself a hot sandwich from deli meat and some sliced Jarlsberg cheese. It looked and smelled amazing, and I could feel myself starting to drool as she took it out of the frying pan.

"Are you standing there because you want to take my food?" Isa asked, sliding the golden-brown sandwich onto a plate, which had two gorgeous red slices of tomato on it.

"No," I replied, although I definitely would have eaten some if she'd offered it.

Isa was a better cook than I was. The only things I could really make were pancakes and cookies. But lately I'd been noticing her making more and more creative snacks in the kitchen. Maybe she would be like our dad and learn to cook a lot of traditional Cuban food.

"Then why are you standing there?" she asked. "You must want something."

I stopped myself before I could sigh. Isa could be so prickly. "I don't want anything," I said nonchalantly. "Well, I was *wondering* something, but it's no big deal."

"Spit it out so I can enjoy my sandwich," she said. She popped open the top of a can of flavored water and took a big sip.

"What do you think of Vista Green middle school?" I asked her.

Isa looked perplexed. "What do *I* think of it? I don't know. Why aren't you asking your BFF Allie?"

"Because she goes there," I said. "I'm just wondering

what most kids at MLK think about Vista Green."

Isa shrugged. "I don't think they think about it at all. Although, I've heard Vista Green has much better food."

"So kids at MLK don't *hate* Vista Green or anything," I said, prodding.

"This is a very weird conversation, even for you, Sierra. Can you please just tell me what you're really asking?"

I couldn't tell her about the student council conversation—that would make me sound like a tattletale, and I'd feel disloyal. Besides, Isa was always looking for opportunities to criticize my activities.

"I overheard someone in the hall today saying that Vista Green was our rival school and this person hated them," I fibbed. "And I wondered if other MLK kids thought that."

Isa looked pensive. "Hmm. I don't know. We do play a lot of big games against them. But we also know a lot of kids there, from youth sports leagues. So the answer is—depends on who you ask."

Her answer made me feel better. Maybe the student council members weren't mean. They just felt a natural rivalry with another school we often played against in sports—a rivalry that I didn't feel, especially since one of my favorite people in the world went there. But the rivalry wasn't inherently bad.

It was a relief. "Thanks, Isa."

"Mm-hmm. Now can you leave so I can eat my sandwich without listening to your stomach grumble?"

I laughed. My stomach *had* been grumbling ever since I'd smelled her sandwich. Probably the next-door neighbors could hear it.

"Fine," I said. "I'm going upstairs to start my math homework. I'll be at your game Thursday, by the way. I moved my meeting."

"Well, la-di-da," she said. "Aren't I the lucky one."

I shook my head as I grabbed my backpack and a granola bar and headed up to my room. Isa could pretend she didn't care all she wanted. I knew the truth. She wanted me at that game, and I wanted to be there. Sisters were sisters, period. Even when they were nonidentical identical twins.

CHAPTER FIVE
GO, ISA!

My parents picked me up from school on Thursday, a rare occurrence, since they were usually at the vet clinic and I usually had after-school activities. But we were headed to Isa's semifinal, and it was in another town about twenty minutes away. I had made a purple-markered GO, ISA! sign the night before and had it with me, as well as a purple bandana to wear in my hair, since her team's colors were purple and silver.

I hoped it would help make up for me forgetting about her game earlier and scheduling a meeting for the same day.

"How did you rearrange your student council meeting?" my mom asked as she steered us onto the parkway.

"It wasn't easy," I replied. "At first everyone was upset, but then I told them if they moved the meeting to Molly's on Sunday when my shift ends, I'd buy them each an ice cream cone with my employee discount!"

"That was sweet of you," said my dad. "I think most meetings would be better with ice cream. Should we try that at the clinic?" he joked to my mother.

My mom nodded, looking thoughtful. "It couldn't hurt. Maybe we'll give you money on Sunday to bring home a few pints in different flavors, Sierra."

"Of course!" I said, happy to have had an idea that not only would be fun for my parents' next staff meeting, but that also supported Molly's. The ice cream shop was still a relatively new business, so every sale mattered.

When we arrived at the soccer field, it was packed. We had to park far away, and when we finally made it to the bleachers, the game had already begun and there was no space to sit three in a row. I let my parents have a small spot in the front, since I knew Isa would want to see their faces. I offered to go look for a separate seat.

The crowd was loud and boisterous. Many parents were wearing Isa's team colors. I had no idea that Isa's semifinal game was *this* big a deal. I was glad I'd brought my purple bandana and my sign.

I walked up a few levels of the bleachers until I found an empty spot that I could squish into. I held up my sign, scanning the field for my sister. She was easy to find, being the only one with a fauxhawk hairstyle, the tips of which she'd sprayed purple for the game. Isa played midfield, and as I watched, she managed to get control of the ball and break away, heading straight for the goal. She was the only girl on the field—the only girl talented enough to try out for an elite all-boys league—and she was faster than everyone chasing her.

I was a decent soccer player, and I really loved playing on a team, but watching my sister's footwork on the field, I knew I'd found another way in which we were not identical. Isa's skills blew mine away. Not only that, but she looked so free and happy as she was running. It was almost like looking at a different person than the sulky one at home. I cheered and hollered for her team until my voice started to get hoarse.

At halftime the score was 2–2, and I stood up to walk over to my parents. As I was making my way down the bleachers, someone grabbed my elbow. I turned around, and it was Lee Murphy from student council.

"Lee! What are you doing here?"

"My cousin plays on the Tigers. You?"

"My sister, Isa, plays midfield on the Panthers," I said proudly.

"That's Isabel Perez? I know her from school. I had no idea she could play like *that*."

I stopped myself from saying "Me too," because I knew it would sound odd.

"Anyway," Lee said, "I'm sort of happy you moved today's council meeting because it meant I could come cheer for Jacob. So thanks for always being so busy."

"You're welcome," I joked. "By the way, do you know what sport Claire plays at school?"

Lee looked at me, confused. "Claire doesn't play a sport. Where did you hear that?"

"Oh," I said, feeling my cheeks turn slightly pink. "I just thought that was the reason why she hates Vista Green so much. You know. We sometimes play big games against them."

Lee laughed and rolled his eyes. "No, that's totally not why Claire hates Vista Green. I can't believe you don't know why. *Everyone* knows. Or, at least, everyone who went to elementary school with Claire, which I did."

I waited for him to go on. I could tell Lee liked having insider information.

"See, Claire used to be best friends with this girl Chloe, all through elementary school. And I mean, best friends. They always went everywhere together, and their names were similar, and they used to dress alike on purpose. People would mix them up, because they were basically attached at the hip. And then when we started middle school, Claire came to MLK and Chloe had to go to Vista Green because her family moved away. And right when sixth grade started, they had some HUGE fight. I don't know what it was about, but they never made up."

I tried to imagine what it would be like to never talk to Allie or Tamiko again. It would be truly terrible.

"That must suck," I said. "Poor Claire."

"Yeah, I know. And I think they run into each other occasionally, but I heard that Chloe won't even *look* at Claire. She just walks right by her."

Claire's feelings about Vista Green definitely made more sense now. Still, it wasn't right to dislike an *entire* school because of one person. I wasn't about to voice my disapproval to Lee, though, so I simply said, "Thanks for telling me. And why don't you like Vista Green?"

Lee shrugged. "I don't have a real reason. I just think Vista Green kids are kind of annoying." Then he lowered his voice, an odd, conspiratorial smile on his face. "You know, I've got a pretty juicy story about Claire and Vikram, too."

Something about the way Lee was so eager to share gossip made me uncomfortable. Would he be gossiping about me next? I didn't want to stick around and find out.

"Uh, thanks, but I need to find my parents and get back to cheering for Isa."

"Yeah, yeah, go. I'm rooting for my cousin's team, obviously, but I still think your sister is great."

Your sister is great.

It was funny. I didn't hear those words very often. At school Isa really removed herself, almost alienated herself, from the crowd I mostly talked to. But out here people could see Isa for who she really was—an amazing athlete.

Although, I suppose her school persona was who she really was too. It was just different from my persona. I wondered if people ever told her how great *I* was, and how that felt. Would it make her proud, jealous, or maybe a bit of both?

I held up my sign and shouted, "GO, ISA," even though it was still halftime and no one was on the field. I just wanted to make sure people knew that the girl with the purple-tipped fauxhawk was my twin.

Isa's team won the game 3–2, and Isa made the assist on the final goal. In the car on the ride home, she was jubilant, bouncing around in her seat and celebrating with a huge purple sports drink and a purple Popsicle. A parent had brought Popsicles for all of the players. "Finals, here we gooo!" she yelled. Isa was so excited that she didn't even bother to complain (again) about how I had *almost* missed the game.

I was thrilled for Isa and her team, and it was fantastic to see her so happy. I hoped her mood would stick around at home. But as much as I wanted to enjoy this rare moment of seeing Isa act like her old self, I couldn't help replaying Lee's and my conversation in my head, over and over again.

The president of our student council had it out for Vista Green, and it wasn't a healthy sports rivalry like I'd hoped it was. She really wanted that Anti–Vista Green Day, and none of the other members seemed to care enough to be against it. I had to make sure it didn't happen, not just because of Allie, but because it was mean, and not what the student council should stand for. And definitely not what Spirit Week should stand for.

I was going to have to come up with more good ideas, and fast.

CHAPTER SIX
ICE CREAM SOUP

It was my favorite day of the week again—Sunday! And this particular Sunday was going to be especially great, because I was going to see Allie and Tamiko at work and then have my postponed student council meeting, where I was going to make *sure* to have so many good ideas for Spirit Week that Claire would completely forget about Anti–Vista Green Day. Plus, it was family dinner night again, and Papi mentioned the day before that he might make his favorite albóndigas—meatballs.

What could be better?

I wore my lucky bright yellow sweater with a jean skirt and ribbed brown tights. Isa always called me "Sunshine" when I wore this sweater, but I didn't care because I was feeling sunshiny, and I knew from experience that a good attitude went a long way.

I practically skipped through the door to Molly's, pleased to be a whopping ten minutes early, something I was rarely able to do. It had to be the power of the yellow sweater.

Allie and Tamiko were already there, and Tamiko was fiddling with the menu up on the wall. Since Mrs. Shear made new ice cream flavors all the time, the menu was a large blackboard so Mrs. Shear could erase and write the new flavors easily. Tamiko was just finishing up adding "Chocolate Chili" to the bottom of the list.

I was a little surprised. I had hoped maybe Mrs. Shear would try it out on some other people who would also think it tasted odd—mixing the spicy with the sweet—but apparently not.

"Looks great!" I told Tamiko, giving her a thumbs-up.

"Thanks!" she replied. "Allie, want to scoop up a photo-ready cone so I can post it on social media and get some chili lovers in here?"

Allie laughed, holding up her right hand, which

already had the ice cream scooper in it. "I'm way ahead of you, Tamiko."

Allie scooped a perfect cone and gave it to me to hold while Tamiko took the picture. I had turquoise nail polish on, which they both thought contrasted nicely with the chocolate ice cream. When the photo had been posted, I stood there, still holding the cone, uncertain what to do with it. We usually just ate the ice cream we used for photos, but I didn't want this one. Nor did I want to *say* I didn't want it.

"Um, should we rock-paper-scissors to see who gets the cone?" I suggested.

Allie giggled. "Sure. Why not?"

We played best out of three, me and Allie and then me and Tamiko, and luckily, Tamiko won. I breathed a sigh of relief as I handed over the cone.

"Mmm, mmm, mmm," Tamiko said, licking the cone. "This really is one of your mom's best, Allie. It's so . . . surprising."

I still couldn't get behind the idea of non-sweet ice cream, but I nodded anyway.

Customers began showing up in groups of twos and threes, as they often did on Sunday afternoons. Sundays had slow foot traffic in the early afternoon, then usually picked up before the evening. It was really busy after dinner, Allie always said, but I didn't work then.

I stood ready at the cash register as three older ladies came in.

They approached the counter, and Tamiko said, "Hello, ladies! Does life seem dull and boring today? How about trying our new Chocolate Chili ice cream? It's sure to liven things up!"

One of the ladies looked shocked for a moment, but then her face broke into a smile, and she said, "You know what? My life could use some livening up. I'll try one!"

"Me too!" said one of the other ladies. The third went for one of my favorite flavors, Peachy Perfection. It was 100 percent peachy sweet. I secretly gave her a thumbs-up.

Tamiko beamed as I rang the orders up, carefully doing the math in my head before I'd let myself hit the total button on the cash register. I took great pride in my ability to add up every order and make change in my head *and* get it right 98 percent of the time.

When a couple came in holding hands a few

minutes later, Tamiko, our marketing maven, immediately pounced.

"Hey there! Looking to spice up your relationship a bit? Try our Chocolate Chili ice cream!"

Allie nudged me, and I covered my mouth with my hand to keep from laughing. How did Tamiko come up with these things? This was why working at Molly's was one of the best parts of my week.

When the couple left (after both ordering Chocolate Chili double scoop cones), Allie said in a fake-scolding voice, "*Tamiko!* Listen, you are doing an awesome job. You are the best salesperson ever! But you can't just promote one flavor, okay? We've got to share the love, or we'll run out of Chocolate Chili too fast."

Tamiko grinned. "I can't help it. It's my favorite. What can I say? The flavor is complex, like me."

Then we all laughed together. Tamiko sold about eight more cones of Chocolate Chili, with her sales pitches getting more and more ridiculous. A few times, I thought Allie was going to get frustrated, but then she couldn't help laughing at Tamiko's ridiculousness and how well it worked.

Too soon I saw that it was almost five o'clock.

That meant my shift was ending and my student council meeting would be starting soon. Lee and Claire arrived together, five minutes early, and grabbed the table that was the farthest from the counter. A few minutes later Hanna arrived, and finally Vikram.

They all came up to get their cones before we started the meeting.

"Great place," said Vikram, looking around. "I haven't been here before."

"Molly's is the best," I told him. "Thanks again for meeting me here. I'm off duty now, so let's get you all your ice cream and we can get started!"

Everyone perused the menu. Claire smiled and said, "It's so perfect that you work at this sweet little ice cream shop, Sierra. Because you're so sweet!"

Vikram nodded. "It's true. This is the perfect job for you." Hanna smiled as well.

I couldn't help blushing. It was nice that they all thought so highly of me. It was also slightly embarrassing to be complimented so publicly. I quickly changed the subject. "What can I get you guys? Anything you want! It's on me."

I was grateful for a 50 percent employee discount.

Otherwise, buying ice cream for the whole council would've emptied my wallet!

"None for me, thanks," said Claire. "Ice cream is mostly unhealthy sugars and fats, you know. I'll just take an ice water, please."

I gawked at her in surprise. The only people I knew who didn't eat ice cream were lactose intolerant and *couldn't* eat it. I simply couldn't imagine not eating something because it had fat in it. Life was too short to *not* eat dessert!

Tamiko, surprisingly, said nothing in response to the fatty ice cream comment and quickly got Claire a cup of ice water and handed it over. Then she said to the others, "Some people say that spicy foods and flavors actually make you *smarter*. So if you're studying or brainstorming, you should try our new Chocolate Chili flavor. It'll keep you awake and alert."

"Really?" said Lee. "I'll try it! Thanks."

"Me too," said Vikram. "Double scoop."

Tamiko beamed.

"Um, if it's okay, I'll have the Peppermint Stick," said Hanna. "Thanks, Sierra."

"Of course it's okay!" I told Hanna. I made myself a scoop of the Peachy Perfection.

Allie and Tamiko got all the cones made while I rang them up and paid for them. Then I took off my apron and clocked out. I was excited for the meeting. Having it at Molly's really did make it feel more fun and special than usual.

Since I was the secretary, I'd brought my note-book with the minutes from the last meeting. I started every meeting by reading aloud the previous meeting's minutes. Only, this time I did something I shouldn't have—I deliberately omitted the Anti–Vista Green Day idea. I was hoping that if I didn't say anything about it and remind everyone, it would just be forgotten. Technically it had gotten discussed at the craft store, not the meeting, so it wasn't totally incorrect to omit it from the minutes. "How about we start with finalizing logistics for the assembly?" I suggested when I was done reading my notes. I knew I was supposed to let Claire lead the meeting, but I was anxious that someone would mention I'd left out something important.

Luckily, everyone was so busy licking their ice creams (and sipping their ice water) that they were barely listening to me. Claire simply said, "Sounds good."

We went over everything we'd need for the assembly, as well as delegating who would make which posters. I offered to do more than my share, since I was eager to keep everyone happy, and also, I liked making posters. It was fun to come up with different designs and color them all in.

After ten or fifteen minutes, we finally made it around to talking about the most important issue— Spirit Week themes. I tapped my foot nervously on the floor and hoped for the best.

"We need to finalize themes ASAP," Claire said. "And we can't just do the same old things this year, right? We want to be different. We want our Spirit Week to be the best ever!"

"Exactly!" I agreed. We did want it to be the best ever. And definitely *not* the meanest ever.

As we were discussing whether or not a Sports Jersey Day was fun or unoriginal, Allie and Tamiko came over to the table.

"You guys—I have a great idea," Tamiko interrupted. I watched nervously as Claire and Lee looked up at her in surprise. "DIY Day! Do it yourself. Everyone can make their own shirt and decorate it however they want. It'll be great! And I don't think any other schools do it, so you don't have to worry about being unoriginal. Sports Jersey Day has been done. Like, many, many times."

Vikram immediately shook his head. "Sierra already pitched that to us last week. We don't have the funds. And it's not *that* original."

"Oh," said Tamiko, sounding hurt.

"Well, *I've* never heard of any school doing it," said Allie, rushing to Tamiko's defense. "Have you also thought about doing a Favorite Book Chara—"

"Listen, your ice cream is *great*, but could you both please not interrupt us?" said Lee. "This is an official student council meeting, even though we had to have it here because of Sierra. Only people who are actual *student council members* get to vote on and decide the Spirit Week themes."

Allie's and Tamiko's jaws dropped open. Mine did too. I couldn't help it. Lee could be so rude sometimes.

"Uh, yeah. Sorry," Allie said quickly, and I could tell she was mortified. Here we were, in her own mother's store, and she was getting yelled at about offering an idea. A *good* idea.

"Anyway," said Lee, his eyes narrowing, "aren't

you Allie Shear? Didn't you move and leave MLK this year? If you don't go to MLK anymore, why do you even *care*?"

Allie's cheeks looked like they were on fire.

"You're not at MLK anymore? Where do you go?" asked Vikram.

Cheeks still flaming, Allie replied, "Vista Green." Her voice was barely more than a whisper.

"*Vista Green?* Are you serious*?*" Claire huffed and looked around the table as if she couldn't believe what she was hearing. "Stop *spying* on our meeting, then."

"Spying?" Tamiko said. "You think she's *spying*?"

Allie shook her head vehemently. "I'm not spying. I was just trying to be helpful. I loved Spirit Week at MLK. Last year Sierra and Tamiko and I—"

But before she could finish, Claire interrupted her. "Please—stop talking. Everyone at Vista Green acts like they're total clones. They all wear the same clothes, same hair, same everything. We don't want our school to become like that. Right, Sierra?"

Everyone turned to look at me—the four other members of the student council and my two best friends. It was my worst nightmare. A worst nightmare for any person who hated conflict. I was being asked to choose sides, something I never, ever wanted to do. I wanted to jump up and defend my best friend, but I also wanted to stay on the student council and not get in trouble for moving our meeting and asking to hold it at Molly's.

I was stuck. I wished I could melt into a pool of ice cream soup and disappear. I would rather have eaten that stupid spicy Chocolate Chili cone than be in this mess.

I opened my mouth, but no words came out. What could I say to make things better *and* not have anyone mad at me?

After a minute Claire slammed her notebook closed with a bang. "Meeting adjourned. We'll meet after school this week—*at school*—where there are no eavesdroppers. We'll vote on the themes then."

Everyone packed up to leave, while I just sat there stupidly, feeling about as small as a piece of dust.

CHAPTER SEVEN
GUILTY

As soon as the student council members were gone, I turned to look at Allie and Tamiko, dying to read their faces. I found only Tamiko standing there.

While the student council members had been packing up and leaving in a huff, several customers had come in, and Allie was busy covering the counter and register. The college student who usually worked after us must have been late.

"We . . . We should go help Allie," I said, jumping to my feet.

"Oh, *now* you want to help her?" said Tamiko angrily. "Why didn't you help her five minutes ago, when she really needed it?"

I shook my head and stared at the wall over

Tamiko's head. It was too hard to look her in the eye.

She slammed her hand on the table. "What is wrong with those people, Sierra? What's wrong with *you*?"

I felt tears pooling in my eyes. I couldn't believe what had just happened. And it had been *all my fault*!

After a few minutes the customers left and Allie finished up at the counter. She came over to where Tamiko and I were facing off.

Tears were steaming down my face now. I wiped them with my napkin, which was sticky with ice cream and probably made me look even more hideous.

"It's okay, Sierra," said Allie. "You don't need to cry. I'm not actually mad at you. I'm more mad at Claire for refusing to eat any ice cream!"

Tamiko snorted. "'Ice cream is mostly unhealthy sugars and fats,'" she mimicked.

"Everything is okay to eat in moderation, unless you have health problems or something," Allie continued. "Anyway, my mom always says that ice cream is good for the soul. So please don't cry, Sierra! I'm not mad!"

Allie's willingness to forgive me was so kind that I almost couldn't take it. I cried harder.

"Allie, I'm so, so, so sorry. I should have said something! I should have stood up for you. You're my best friend!"

"I know," said Allie. "And I know you feel miserable. That's why I forgive you. I know it's hard for you to be in situations like that."

I was so racked with guilt, it felt like I'd been poisoned with it. I could feel the guilt seeping through my body. I cared so much about my Sprinkle Sundays friendships. They were an important part of who I was. But what kind of person was I if I couldn't stand up for my two best friends?

"You're too nice for your own good," said Tamiko. "You need some backbone."

"Oh, Tamikoooo," I sobbed.

"Well, you do," she replied. "I'm not as forgiving as Allie—sorry. I don't understand why you're on student council with those people. With that *Claire*."

I wiped my face again. "You know, Claire is actually really nice. And organized. She does a good job running the council. I mean, she's nice until you mention Vista Green."

Tamiko crossed her arms over her chest. "Seriously? She doesn't seem nice *at all*, Sierra. Are you completely oblivious?"

I shook my head. "No, I'm not. I know she was awful just now. But, see, she had this best friend, and they did everything together in elementary school, just like us! And then they split up to go to different middle schools, and her friend went to Vista Green. Anyway, they had some huge fight and never spoke again, and I think her heart is kind of broken over it. You know, her friendship heart."

"Like how we would feel if we weren't friends anymore," said Allie quietly. "I see why she would be upset. I guess her comments had nothing to do with me, and everything to do with her friend."

"It's sad when friendships fall apart," said Tamiko. "But that isn't going to happen to us."

And then she pulled me and Allie into a group hug, which was extremely kind, since I didn't feel I deserved it at all.

"I'm going to make it up to you guys," I blubbered. "I don't know how, but I will."

"You don't need to make anything up to us," Allie declared.

Tamiko, however, launched into another rant.

"Honestly, Sierra, I didn't like any of them. Lee and Vikram were mean too. Lee told me to butt out! I'm a student at MLK. Just because I'm not on the student council doesn't mean my thoughts don't matter. And they were jerks about my DIY idea, which I *know* is awesome."

"Lee *is* odd," I agreed. "He can be super-nice and chatty sometimes, but then really mean. I've noticed that. But he's an excellent treasurer. He's so careful with the money. And Vikram always has good ideas. . . ." I let my voice trail off as I watched Allie's and Tamiko's faces fall. Here they were, supporting me and hugging me and forgiving me after I had just royally let them down, allowing the student council to insult Allie in her own family store. And now I was standing up for those very people who'd insulted her.

Why was I defending people I barely knew and wasn't really friends with (nor would I want to be), when I couldn't even stand up and defend Allie when I needed to?

Tamiko saw the expression on my face and nodded. "You know you need to quit that awful student council, right?" she said. "I know you like being on it, but those kids aren't nice, Sierra. It isn't worth hanging out with mean people."

I thought about our last few meetings, and how worried I was about Twin Day and Anti–Vista Green Day. Tamiko was right. I wasn't actually enjoying student council this year. And I didn't *have* to do it. I chose to. So I could choose not to.

"You know, I think you're right. I should quit."

Allie's face lit up. "Really? Wow. That would be a big deal for you, Sierra. You never quit anything."

"I know," I said, "but I already know it's the right thing to do because just saying it out loud has made me feel a little bit better."

Allie hugged me again, and I knew how lucky I was to have a friend like her. She was the truly sweet one, not me.

I headed home, mulling over in my head my conversation with my friends. It had been easy to agree with Allie and Tamiko that I should quit student council, but I knew it would be a whole other ball game to have to march into a meeting and quit to Claire's face. What if she freaked out and yelled at me? Or told me I couldn't quit because I had to finish the year? I hated confronting people and giving anyone any reason to be mad at me.

Even worse, what if Claire said mean things about me at school? And told everyone I was a quitter or a jerk? Based on her attitude about her ex-friend Chloe, Claire seemed like she would hold grudges.

Everyone at MLK thought I was kind and sweet and hardworking. I didn't want to lose that reputation. And there was no denying that I cared about my reputation—a lot. I wanted to be liked.

As soon as I walked into my house, I could smell Papi's cooking. I was glad once again that I could enjoy eating ice cream and albóndigas without constantly worrying about fat. Food was one of the best parts of life, my parents said, and I agreed with them.

"Dinner will be in ten minutes!" Papi called as I headed upstairs to drop off my bag with my student council notes.

I passed Isa's door on the way, and as usual it was shut tight. I paused, my fist shooting up and knocking on it almost instinctively.

"Who is it?" she grumbled.

"Can I come in?" I asked, shaking my head. Honestly. Couldn't she just say "Come in"? There were only three people it could be—me, Mami, or Papi.

"I guess."

I opened the door and walked in. Isa had a candle burning that smelled powdery and strange. I didn't like it, but I didn't say anything. One of our cats, Cinnamon, was curled up on her bed, and Isa was drawing in a sketch pad.

"Isa, am I too nice?" I asked her.

Isa's eyes popped open wide. "Do you even have to ask? Yes, you are. Nice and sunny, that's you." And she pointed at my yellow sweater.

Isa always said exactly what was on her mind, with no apologies to anyone. She didn't try hard to make everyone like her—she didn't care if they did. She was just unabashedly herself, take it or leave it.

It wasn't always easy to live with, but especially after everything that had happened at Molly's that day, I sort of admired her bluntness.

"Why *are* you asking?" Isa said.

"It's just that . . . well, I sort of envy how you can be so gruff and blunt with everyone. And no one thinks less of you. They just think, *Well, that's Isa.* But if I were to act like that, they'd say I was mean." I fiddled awkwardly with my hair. "It's pretty cool how you can just . . . be you."

Isa looked surprised. She cleared her throat. "Being nice *is* you just being you. You actually *are* nice, Sierra. That's not a bad thing."

"I know it's not. But you see . . . I was in a situation where someone said something really mean to Allie, and I froze. I couldn't even speak up and defend her! Because I didn't want that other person to think I was a jerk."

"Standing up for your best friend doesn't make you a jerk," Isa said. "Why don't you stop worrying so much about what everyone else is thinking?"

"Okay."

"You'll be fine," Isa said.

"Okay."

"Now leave me alone so I can finish this drawing before dinner."

I grinned. Isa had just illustrated my point. She was never afraid to say exactly what she wanted when she wanted to. Most people would never tell me to leave them alone. But my sister would.

"Thanks. Team P forever?" I said, raising my hand for a fist bump.

"Yeah, yeah," Isa said, but she ignored my raised hand.

Fist bump rejected, I left her room and closed the door, heading to my own room to change into sweats before dinner. As I did, I tossed my yellow sweater into the corner of the closet, where I hopefully wouldn't see it again for a while. It certainly hadn't been lucky that day.

CHAPTER EIGHT
A DEFLATED BALLOON

It's one thing to make a decision in your head, but it's another thing to actually carry it out.

When I got to school on Monday, I resolved to quit the student council the first chance I got. But even though I saw Claire in the hallway a number of times, I couldn't make myself go up to her and tell her. I pictured the look of disappointment, and probably anger, on her face. I'd be leaving her with no council secretary. I felt guilty and irresponsible.

Someone else could have gotten this position and really enjoyed it. What was wrong with me? *Was* something wrong with me?

So even though I passed Claire at least three times, I just smiled and walked on without saying anything.

On Tuesday at lunch, I sat with Tamiko and MacKenzie, one of our friends who'd transferred to MLK this year. I was sitting only inches from my friends, but my mind was far away, worrying about my to-do list.

"It's my favorite week of the year," Tamiko was saying to MacKenzie. "You get to dress up, and there are bake sales, and an assembly and a pep rally. It's the best."

"So what are the themes this year, Sierra?" MacKenzie asked me.

"For what?" I said. I'd only been half listening to their conversation. The last thing I remembered was . . . Tamiko saying *Science quiz tomorrow.*

"Spirit Week," MacKenzie said. "Since I wasn't here last year, I don't know how it usually works at MLK."

Ugh. Spirit Week. I couldn't escape it! That was what the whole school was thinking about. When would the student council announce the themes so that everyone could start planning their costumes and everything? Claire had texted that morning and organized a meeting for Friday, which was the soonest date that all of us could make it. We were going to hold the final vote at that meeting.

I knew I should quit before then, but part of me reasoned it would be smarter to stay, so I could vote against Anti–Vista Green Day. If I had the power to stop that theme, I thought I should try.

"Um, we still haven't decided on the themes," I said to MacKenzie. "We're voting on Friday."

"You mean *they're* voting on Friday," said Tamiko. "Because you're quitting student council ASAP, right, Sierra?"

I frowned at her and sent secret eye signals telling her to knock it off. I didn't want to explain the whole mess to MacKenzie, and I didn't appreciate Tamiko bringing it up in front of her. I didn't need MacKenzie thinking less of me too.

Tamiko rolled her eyes. "I know you so well, Sierra. You're doubting yourself. You're wondering if you should quit, and what will happen, and will everyone hate you? I get it. It's not fun to quit something midyear. But being on that council is making you unhappy, and *less nice*. That's not right. Spend your time on activities and people that make you feel *good* about yourself."

"It's not that," I said quickly, even though she was

dead-on. "I *am* planning to quit. I just haven't had the right minute to tell Claire yet, and I don't want it getting around school first."

MacKenzie looked stricken. "I wouldn't tell anyone, Sierra. Honestly."

"I know you wouldn't," I said. "But let's stop talking about it anyway. *Okay?*" I emphasized the last word, looking pointedly at Tamiko.

"Okaaaay," she replied. "Do you want to talk about this slab of dog food that passes as a hamburger here instead?" She held up her lunch from the cafeteria, and I had to agree—it didn't look appetizing.

"Maybe Vista Green kids *are* snobs," she joked, "but only because they've been spoiled by having edible food."

"My brother's best friend goes to Vista Green," said MacKenzie. "He's really nice."

"See? There you go," said Tamiko. What point she was trying to make exactly, I didn't understand, but I got her meaning well enough.

"I'll do it, Tamiko," I said. "I. Will. Do. It."

"It might help if you stop thinking of it as quitting," Tamiko added. "You're resigning. Because of creative differences. It happens all the time in the fashion world."

I burst into laughter. Tamiko had an answer for everything! She was a good friend, and a good person. She would never want to have an Anti–Vista Green Day, even if Allie didn't go there. And she would never let someone talk her into voting for it either.

In my mind I continued to run through how I would resign. At soccer practice I worried; at band practice I worried; during music and Spanish and math class I worried.

I truly hated being at the center of conflict. I loved being a teammate and a team player. I loved working hard and doing lots of activities and doing them all well. Quitting just wasn't in my nature.

When Friday finally crawled around, I was a jittery wreck. I hadn't slept well the night before. I had Isa's bluntness in my head, and Tamiko's sharp words, and Allie's wonderful forgiving hug from the other day. It was all just one big jumble. Even my feet and hands were twitchy, like my mom when she drinks too much coffee.

I resolved to arrive early to the meeting and tell Claire privately that it would be my last meeting. Then I would offer to still help with the posters. That way I could feel good about not shoving my work off onto other people.

But my plan fell apart when my last class of the day, biology, ran five minutes over, and I had to dash to my locker to get the student council notebook and then run to room 215B. When I finally made it, the other members were all there, waiting for me as usual. I felt so guilty about being late that I just plopped down into my seat and kept my mouth shut.

There was no way I was resigning in front of Lee, Hanna, and Vikram.

"I guess we can begin now," said Claire. "Read the notes, please, Sierra?"

I opened the notebook and read the notes from the disastrous meeting at Molly's. Obviously, I'd left out the ugly parts and only written down actual business items.

"And then we were spied on," Lee chimed in when I finished.

Vikram laughed. "That *was* weird."

"You can't trust a Vista Green kid—even a friend," Claire said with a look in my direction. "You're so nice, Sierra, that you probably don't even realize how mean and sneaky other people can be. Everyone likes you, so you like everyone."

I couldn't help being flattered by her compliments. It was nice to be liked. But I also knew that the rest of what she was saying was very wrong.

Claire went on. "But we're in safe territory now, so let's hurry up and vote on the Spirit Week themes so we can announce them and make the posters. Everyone has been asking me about it for days."

I nodded. I was ready to get the vote over with too. And then the resigning.

We started by writing our options on the whiteboard and crossing out some of the ones that were obvious duds.

"I think Monday should be Crazy Hair Day," Vikram suggested. "That way we can start small with the themes, and then have them build and get bigger as we head toward Friday, which should definitely be Red and Gold Day."

"I agree," I said quickly, wanting to be positive before I had to be negative. "I love Crazy Hair Day, and it's nice to have one that people don't have to find a special outfit for."

We went around the circle, and the idea passed unanimously.

The vote for Tuesday went smoothly as well, with

Lee suggesting we do Pajama Day, which was a perennial favorite with both students and teachers.

I voted eagerly for that one too. Hope started to bloom in my chest. Maybe everything would be okay. Maybe I wouldn't have to quit.

Then we were voting on the Wednesday theme, and Hanna suggested Twin Day, with a nervous look in my direction. Did she know how much I didn't want it? Or did she think she was suggesting something I'd like?

"We did Twin Day last year," I said quickly. "Don't we want to do some different things this year? How about a Dress as Your Future Self Day, and people can dress like the career they want to have?"

Vikram shook his head. "We want to do *popular* things, not necessarily different things. And last year's Twin Day was a huge success."

"Anyway," Lee chimed in, "you should be voting FOR it, Sierra. You have an awesome fraternal twin. Your sister is one of the best middle school soccer players I've ever seen."

"We're identical, actually," I said quietly.

"You *are*?" said Claire in disbelief. "You'd never know it. Your sister is so dark and moody. And you're

75

so sunny and sweet. Everyone loves you."

Was she saying that everyone *didn't* love Isa? I knew that was probably true, but why say that about my twin sister right to my face?

"Wait, is that why you don't want to do Twin Day? You don't like your twin or something?" Vikram asked.

His words caught me completely off guard. I couldn't believe someone would accuse me of something like that—that I didn't like my own *twin*.

"That's ridiculous," I said. I tried to keep my voice steady, even though I wanted to shout in his face. "I love my sister."

"Doesn't sound like it," said Vikram.

"*Of course* she loves her sister, Vikram," said Claire, rolling her eyes. "You're so weird. C'mon. Let's vote. All in favor of Twin Day, with one of our own as an actual identical twin?"

I was stuck. I really, really, really didn't want to have Twin Day, but I also knew that if I voted against it now, they would all think it was because I didn't want to dress alike with Isa. They wouldn't understand the real reason, which was that I didn't want to hurt Isa or Tamiko by choosing one over the other, because I loved them both so much.

I raised my hand and voted yes. How had I gotten into this mess? And why hadn't I gotten myself out yet? I didn't know what to do.

Finally it was the moment of truth. We only had one day left—Thursday—since Friday was already going to be Red and Gold Day.

I spoke up quickly. "How about we do Famous Couples Day?" I suggested. "That hasn't been done before."

"Too much like Twin Day," said Lee. "You need a partner."

"Well, Celebrity Day, then. That'd be neat, right? Everyone would love to be a celebrity for a day."

"Yeah, but it's not very school-spirited," said Vikram. "We should do Anti–Vista Green Day. We can dress like clones and complain about everything. It'll be great."

"Yeah, I agree," said Claire. "All in favor, say 'Aye.'"

I heard several voices shout "AYE!" It didn't even matter that I hadn't spoken, because the other voices were so loud.

"Any nays?" asked Claire. She started writing the final choices in her notebook so that she could make the announcement to students on Monday.

This was it. I'd missed my moment to speak up on Sunday, but here was the opportunity again. I could say, "No, we need a less mean-spirited theme" or "How about something more fun?" or, well, anything.

But I kept picturing everyone being angry with me as I spoke, and thinking I was difficult. I pictured them saying that I didn't like my sister, and I loved Vista Green, and maybe I should just go *there*. And all the courage I had been working up since Sunday deflated like a week-old Spirit Week balloon.

Pppppfffft.

I said nothing. It was like my lips and throat were glued shut.

"Anti–Vista Green Day it is," said Claire, banging her pen on the table like a gavel. "You got all that, Sierra? Let's get to work on those posters. I want them up first thing Monday morning."

CHAPTER NINE

SINGING OUR TRUTHS

My mom had to be at the vet clinic all day Saturday, but my dad was home. He offered to drive me to band practice, since he was already taking Isa to soccer. It was her last practice before her team headed to the finals the following week. Even though Isa hadn't said anything about it to me, I knew she was nervous. I'd heard her kicking the ball around in the backyard the past few days, trying to shoot it past the obstacle my mom had fixed up for her—a piece of plywood with several holes cut out. The holes were so she could aim to get the ball into the goal in places where the goalie might not be able to stop it.

"Is your team ready for finals?" I asked her.

Isa shrugged and looked out the car window, in

the opposite direction of me. "As ready as we're going to be."

"I think you guys will win," I said. "You really are great."

"So is the other team, Sierra," she replied, as if I didn't know that. "That's why we're both in the finals."

"Um, right," I said.

Isa pressed on, as if she were talking to a very small child who knew nothing about soccer, instead of her twin who played on the girls' team at school. "And the other team's been undefeated all season. We've lost two games."

"Well, *I* think you're ready," I said, unsure of how else to respond.

Isa shook her head at me, as if I were telling her they would all become astronauts and go to the moon after the game.

I caught my dad's eye in the rearview mirror. He smiled knowingly. Sometimes it was so hard to give Isa a compliment, or to just chat with her.

"Sierra," he said, "whatever happened with your Spirit Week themes? You didn't tell us."

At this, Isa turned to look at me with interest. We weren't announcing them officially at school until

Monday, but Isa wasn't exactly the type to text-blast the information to her friends. She was more likely to pretend it *wasn't* Spirit Week and not dress up at all, because dressing up would be too conventional. So why did she even care?

I cleared my throat. It was embarrassing just saying them out loud, because I was so unhappy about it. "Crazy Hair Day, Pajama Day, Twin Day, Anti–Vista Green Day, and Red and Gold Day," I hurriedly spat out, letting all the words run together.

"Oh goody," said Isa. "*Twin Day*. I'll be you and you'll be me."

She stared at me, waiting to see what I'd say, but I didn't react. I'd already promised Tamiko I'd dress up with her. Was Isa serious, or was she just testing me?

"What's this Anti–Vista Green Day?" asked Papi. "You mean Allie's school?"

I nodded miserably. "Yes. I didn't vote for it, Papi. MLK apparently thinks Vista Green is full of clones and snobs."

"That's silly," said Isa.

"It *is* silly," said my dad. "I'm surprised you couldn't think of something more positive, Sierra. That isn't like you at all."

"Can we change the subject?" I asked.

"No need," said my dad cheerfully. "You're here! Have a good practice. I'll pick you up around five."

"Thanks," I said, climbing out of the car.

"Can't wait to dress up together, Twin!" Isa called out as I closed the door.

Arrgh!

It was a huge relief to walk into Reagan's garage, where I was fairly certain we would spend 99 percent of the next few hours playing and talking about music, not discussing Spirit Week.

Reagan, Tessa, and Kasey were already there, and Kasey was playing a song on the keyboard. Tessa was humming along with it softly, and Reagan was playing air-drums with her drumsticks.

"That's a great melody!" I said. "I don't know that song. What is it?"

Tessa shook back her long dirty-blond hair and laughed. "Of course you don't know it! I just wrote it last night."

"You did?" Tessa never failed to impress me. She played guitar, sang, and wrote songs. She was super-talented.

Tessa nodded. "Mm–hmm. And I'm really glad you like it, because I wrote it with you in mind!"

"Me?" I was floored. "Why would you write a song about *me*?"

"Because it's a ballad about friendship. I realized that I've written so many songs about romantic love, but what about friendship? So I started thinking about all of my friends, and I thought of you, and how incredibly nice and sweet you are—"

"*UUUUGHHHH*," I blurted out without thinking. Tessa looked stricken, and I immediately felt embarrassed by my reaction.

Reagan looked concerned. "What's wrong, Sierra?"

"It's just . . . well, the song is beautiful, Tessa. And it's amazing that you're writing a song about friendship, and you thought of *me*, and all that stuff. I'm so flattered! It's just lately I've been wondering whether or not it's really a good thing to be sweet."

"What do you mean?" asked Kasey. She was still playing the melody softly on the keyboard, and it was starting to gnaw at me. I could hear now how sweet the tune was. Sweet and spineless, like me.

"I'm not sure that being a sweet girl is a good thing," I said, wondering how on earth I was going to explain what I meant without getting into the whole Spirit Week debacle. I didn't want these girls to be disappointed in me too. I already knew I needed to break the bad news to Allie and Tamiko before the themes became public at school on Monday.

"I think you're *all* sweet girls," said Reagan's mom, coming into the garage carrying a tray of lemonade and pretzel sticks. "And talented, too."

"Thanks, Mom," said Reagan, looking slightly uncomfortable. I knew I'd feel the same way if my mom jumped into a conversation I was having with my friends, but I was feeling desperate for advice. So maybe Mrs. Leone was a good option.

"Mrs. Leone, what should a 'sweet girl' do when she wants to disagree with someone? When you want to say how you feel but you can't, because you're not sweet if you disagree with people?"

"Why not?" asked Kasey.

"Yes, I agree," said Mrs. Leone. "You can disagree and still be sweet. Haven't you ever heard the saying 'You catch more flies with honey than with vinegar'? It means that you're more likely to get what you want if you're nice about it. But you should still speak your mind. Do it nicely and politely, and people will still respect you and listen to you."

I sipped my lemonade and thought about what she was saying. What if in the meeting on Friday I'd just said, "Hey, guys, Anti–Vista Green Day seems mean to me. How about we pick something more positive to do instead?" I had made other suggestions, but I hadn't come right out and just *said* how I felt about things.

Mrs. Leone was staring at me, as if waiting for an answer. "Maybe you're right," I said finally.

"Don't even worry about not being sweet, Sierra," said Kasey. "Just be YOURSELF and you'll be fine. And if yourself disagrees with someone, that's okay. You should always let your voice be heard!"

"Isn't that why we're in a band?" asked Reagan, giggling. "To sing our truths? To make music we believe in?"

"Now you've got it," said Mrs. Leone with a wink. She left, and I turned to look at Tessa, who'd been silent this whole time, not even taking a cup of lemonade. She was scribbling furiously in her notebook.

"What are you writing now, Tessa?" I asked her.

"Oh, you know, lyrics," she replied. "This is all great stuff we're talking about. I don't want you to sing something you're not feeling, so I'm changing up the friendship song to make it better. This is a song for *you*, Sierra, and I'm going to make sure it suits you. And if it doesn't, TELL ME and I'll fix it! Don't just smile and say you like it. I want to hear what you think."

I laughed. Tessa was such a great person. So talented, so creative, but also nice! She could be shy when she wasn't playing or talking about music, but she didn't seem to have trouble standing up for herself. She was pretty cool.

I was incredibly touched that she'd not only write a song about me but *rewrite* it to better fit me. I couldn't wait to hear her new version. Would it be sweet? Sour? Spicy? Or the right combination of all three?

"Listen, this has all been very enlightening, but we should probably practice or no one is ever going to listen to any of our songs because we'll play them all so badly," said Reagan. She picked up her drumsticks and sat down at her drums. "C'mon, Wildflowers. Are we ready to rock or not?"

She went straight into a fast song that got my blood pumping and my feet moving as I sang. And it was either the fun of singing and hanging out with my band, or just the upbeat melody of the song, but almost instantly I felt better.

Was it possible to stop being just sweet and start being Sierra?

CHAPTER TEN
SIERRA THE SCAREDY-CAT

For once, I was dreading going to Molly's. I'd *never* dreaded going to work (after all, I worked in an ice cream parlor!), and I'd definitely never dreaded getting to spend time with my two best friends, one of whom I mostly only saw on Sundays. But I knew Tamiko and Allie would ask me about whether I'd quit student council, and I couldn't bear to tell them how I'd chickened out.

I wore one of my loudest outfits—a bright orange striped knit sweater with a pair of jeans and my bright orange high-tops—hoping the *outfit* would be a conversation piece instead of *me*.

"Whoa!" said Tamiko, holding up a hand and pretending to shield her eyes when I walked in.

"It's so bright in here. . . . Is it the sun?"

"Haha," I said, pretending to sound offended but secretly thrilled that my plan was working. "I was just feeling like some orange today, that's all."

"*Some* orange is one thing. That's a whole LOT of orange," Tamiko joked.

"Don't listen to her," said Allie loyally. "Your hair always looks so good with bright colors! I wish I could wear them."

"You can!" I told her. "Anyone can."

"Not like you," she replied.

I shook my head. Allie was much too modest. It was then that I noticed Allie was holding a small blackboard. She held it up for me to see. It read:

The Benefits of Eating Ice Cream

- Includes vitamins A, B6, B12, C, D, and E!
- Provides energy to fuel your day!
- Stimulates a happiness hormone in the brain!
- Different flavors make every day exciting!
- Good for the soul! ☺

She moved the board to rest on the ledge over the register so that customers could see it while they were checking out the flavors.

"Claire made me so mad the other day," she explained. "Imagine someone *not* eating ice cream! It's obviously not a health food, but I don't want people feeling guilty when they eat ice cream. I had to do something, so I did a little research."

"I like it," I said. "There's no denying that ice cream is good for the soul!"

"I love the sign," said Tamiko. "Want me to post a picture of it on social media?"

Allie's face broke into a huge smile. "Would you? That would be great!"

Tamiko took a few pictures, played with the filters, and then posted one online. "There! That'll show all the ice cream haters out there. Or, the one hater we know."

I was starting to get nervous. All this talk about Claire meant we were only seconds away from one of them bringing up the council and the thing that I didn't do this week.

Luckily, I was saved by the beautiful warm weather. Not two seconds later a group of five high school girls came in, then a woman carrying a tiny Yorkie puppy, and then a steady stream of other customers followed. The three of us were busy filling orders and keeping up with whatever elaborate specials Tamiko felt like inventing, like her Good for the Soul Shake, which was a blend of the customer's four favorite flavors. It was an interesting idea—which worked out well sometimes, but sometimes the end result was really odd and just didn't taste good at all.

Time was flying, and I couldn't have been more relieved. But all good things must come to an end, I guess.

"I've been meaning to ask," Tamiko began. But before she could get the words out, I turned my back to her and began viciously wiping the countertops with a rag. The expression on my face was so guilty, I had to hide it.

"How did Claire take it when you quit the other day?" she asked.

This was it. I had to admit the truth—I hadn't done it.

But still, the words wouldn't come. A second went by. Then another.

"Sierra?" said Allie.

I turned around to face Tamiko and Allie. "I didn't get the chance," I finally admitted. "Our meeting was so busy, and I got there last. So I couldn't quit."

There was a slight pause. "You don't mean you *couldn't* quit," said Tamiko. "You mean you *didn't* quit."

Ouch. That stung. Tamiko was right, though. There had been opportunities for me to say something to Claire all week. I was the one who'd decided to wait until the meeting on Friday and then had gotten there last. I had procrastinated and then had just given up. I hadn't been brave enough to speak up . . . again.

Sierra the scaredy-cat.

I didn't even try to defend myself. I just fidgeted with a container of paper straws for the milkshakes.

Tamiko came to stand beside me. "It's okay, Sierra. You can do this! You really can. Just get your phone out and send Claire a text. Do it now. You'll feel better!"

"A text? I can't tell her over text. That's not very mature or responsible," I said. What would quitting over text do to my reputation? "I have to do it in person."

Allie looked sympathetically at me. "I agree, Sierra. In person is best. Or call her. But you need to do it."

I nodded. "I know. I will."

Tamiko asked, "Did you get to help vote on the themes at least? Are they any good?"

My cheeks flamed red. This was getting worse and worse. I felt like such a disappointment to my friends, and yet it was *Claire* that I kept worrying I would disappoint.

"Um, yeah. We voted. The themes are Crazy Hair Day, Pajama Day, Twin Day, Anti–Vista Green Day, and Red and Gold Day." I tried to keep my tone neutral as I said the words aloud. It was still hard to believe that these themes had been my decisions too. I had participated in the voting, and I hadn't fought against Anti–Vista Green Day, which was basically the same as voting yes.

Instead of the reaction I'd expected, however, which was that Allie would respond in horror to Anti–Vista Green Day, she quickly said, "Are you and Tamiko going to dress up together for Twin Day?"

There was a strange tone to her voice that I didn't recognize.

"Is that even a question?" Tamiko replied, grinning. "*Of course* we are."

Were we? But what if Isa had been serious the

other day about dressing up with me? She had clearly been hurt by me "triplet-ing" with Tamiko and Allie the year before. What if Twin Day really did mean something to her? I couldn't let Isa down again.

Tamiko could always dress up with MacKenzie if necessary. But Isa didn't have another twin.

I didn't respond, and Tamiko noticed. Her smile quickly turned to a frown.

Just then a young man came into the shop. He worked at the grocery store across the street and was one of our regular customers. He immediately noticed Allie's new blackboard and started laughing. "Good for the soul," he read aloud. "I love it!"

"Thank you," Allie responded, but I couldn't help noticing that her smile seemed forced. And when her head was bent over the tubs of ice cream, her mouth was pinched down in a frown.

Oh no. I suddenly realized why Allie was upset too. If Tamiko and I dressed up as twins, she'd be left out because she was at a different school. It had been our "thing" together the year before—the three of us—and now she couldn't be a part of that.

I nervously glanced over at Tamiko, who was happily pitching the Chocolate Chili ice cream to an intrigued customer. She hadn't seemed to notice that Allie was upset. If I dressed up with Isa so that Allie wouldn't feel left out, Tamiko would be sad.

I wanted to start scooping ice cream with my hands and throw it at the walls. Spirit Week, which was supposed to be one of the highlights of the school year, was turning into a complete and utter disaster.

And I was to blame, because I hadn't been brave enough to stop it from spinning out of control.

I had been trying so hard to be sweet. But why was that making everything around me sour?

CHAPTER ELEVEN
SUGAR AND SPICE

On Sunday night, despite Tamiko's and Allie's disappointment in me, and *my* disappointment in myself, I went ahead and made all the Spirit Week posters I'd signed up to do. After all, I'd promised to do them, and not making the posters wasn't going to change how the vote had gone. It would just make me look lazy.

I got to school early Monday morning and hung the posters in the halls. I tried to avoid running into anyone and kept my head down as I worked. Not so long ago, I was proud to be on the student council. How had it all changed so fast?

Even before the first bell rang, everyone was talking about Anti–Vista Green Day. I overheard some kids saying they liked it, and some who said they were confused by it. I guess I wasn't the only one who had no idea that MLK students were "supposed" to dislike Vista Green, although that fact didn't make me feel much better.

I avoided Claire all day, knowing I still didn't have the guts to quit the council. Tamiko thankfully said nothing at lunch, just raised her eyebrows when MacKenzie mentioned I'd done a nice job on the posters. I changed the subject and got Tamiko talking about how she planned to repaint her nightstand that weekend.

Luckily, I had my Wildflowers practice to go to after school, which would hopefully distract me from my big fat mess. But as soon as I got there, Tessa said, "Sierra! I've been dying to talk to you all day. What's the deal with Anti–Vista Green Day? Everyone's talking about it. I can't believe you'd vote for that—especially since Colin and Allie go there."

Tessa knew Allie through me, but she'd met Colin at the pool the previous summer, and had a pretty serious crush on him. In fact, a couple of her songs were even about him. So I could see why Anti–Vista Green Day would particularly bother her.

97

"Yeah, Sierra," said Kasey. "It's not like you at all."

They were right, but I felt so guilty that I immediately became defensive. "It wasn't *me*. It was the whole council! Everyone votes. I kept suggesting other ideas, but . . ." My voice trailed off. I was hoping they wouldn't ask if I'd actually stood up and said, "No, that's a bad idea." Because I hadn't.

Reagan must have noticed how uncomfortable I felt, because she picked up her drumsticks and said, "Should we get started, girls? I've got a big algebra test to study for tonight."

I caught her eye and smiled gratefully, then took my place at the mic. We always started with a few familiar warm-up songs before moving on to practice new ones. But even though I'd sung the warm-ups many, many times before, my brain refused to cooperate. I missed my cues, I forgot the words, and at one point I just botched an entire refrain.

"You're not on beat, Sierra," Kasey called out. She was trying to be helpful, but I knew I wasn't on beat. I wasn't on key, either.

"Ughhh, sorry," I said. "Let's try it again."

Finally, after the fourth painful slog through a song I should have known as well as "Happy Birthday to

You," Reagan put down her drumsticks and stood up.

"You know what I think we need?" she said. "A break. I'll be right back."

And she left the garage and headed toward her house.

"I'm sorry I'm so off today, guys," I mumbled to Tessa and Kasey. "I don't know what's wrong with me."

"It's okay," said Tessa. "I have days like that too."

Reagan reappeared, carrying bowls, spoons, and a tub of Molly's ice cream. "You guys *have* to try this new flavor—Chocolate Chili! It's the best. I asked my mom to buy three cartons."

Kasey and Tessa crowded around her. "Chocolate Chili? Sounds awesome!" said Kasey. "Did you help invent this one, Sierra?"

"No. It was all Mrs. Shear," I said limply, feeling silly that I hadn't spoken up to Mrs. Shear about not liking this flavor either. Mrs. Shear had given it to me to taste-test and had specifically requested my honest feedback. But instead I'd just said what I thought she wanted to hear, to be nice. What was the point of having opinions if I didn't *say* them?

Tessa tried the ice cream and pretended to faint. "Oh my goodness—this is incredible! I love how it's not *just* sweet. It tastes . . . exciting, and interesting, and fun!"

"Kind of like Colin?" teased Reagan.

Tessa blushed. "Haha," she said, looking down at her ice cream.

Kasey jumped in to save Tessa. "It's neat how the chili spice doesn't take anything away from the chocolate. It just makes it better."

I was skeptical about trying this flavor again. I hadn't liked it at all before. But watching my bandmates enjoy it, and remembering how much Allie and Tamiko had liked it, I figured, why not? After all, ice cream was good for the soul, according to Allie's blackboard.

I took a tentative bite, and it was just as I remembered it—confusing! Sweet, then spicy, then sweet again. But as I took a few more bites, trying to avoid making conversation, I started to get used to it.

It even started to taste okay to me.

Maybe it would be *boring* if ice cream was always just sweet. Maybe a bit of spice *didn't* hurt the sweetness in an ice cream flavor. Or a person. Maybe it just made it more interesting, and in a good way.

Maybe I'd been trying a little too hard lately to

protect my sweet, perfect reputation. Why not add some chili to Sierra?

When everyone had finished their bowl, we got up and headed over to our instruments to get back to practicing.

"Guess what, guys?" said Tessa, waving a few sheets of paper in her hands. "I finished my new song! I've been waiting to show it to you until it was ready."

"Already?" I asked. "How?"

"I had a lot of inspiration," she said, smiling at me. "Here. Take a look."

"What's the title?" I asked as she was handing the sheets around.

"I'm not sure—but after trying that awesome ice cream flavor, I'm thinking 'Sugar and Spice.'"

"I like that," said Kasey. "

"Okay. Here goes. I'll just play the melody and sing it for you one time, and then Sierra can *really* sing it."

Tessa picked up her guitar and positioned the music in front of her. In her lovely, soft voice, she started singing:

> *"Some people say that girls should be good,*
> *But I say, what good does that do a girl?*

Stand up, speak up, say what's on your mind.
It's time for girls to stop being just kind!

Some people say that girls should be good,
But I say, what good does that do a girl?
Stand up, speak up, to whomever you meet.
It's time for girls to stop being just sweet!"

When Tessa finished, I found myself applauding. There were tears in my eyes. Her song was so exactly right. It was everything I'd been wanting to say over the past few weeks, yet had been unable to be brave enough to.

I went to Tessa and threw my arms around her in a hug, almost squashing her guitar between us. "Thank you, Tessa. That song is *perfect*. You don't know how much I need it right now! I can't wait to learn it and really perform it."

Tears immediately sprang to Tessa's eyes as well. "This is why I wrote it! Sierra, you are *so* sweet and kind. And I know how hard it is to speak up. I'm so shy at school! It's really hard sometimes. But writing this song helped me."

"I think a song like this can help all of us," said

Reagan. "It's a great reminder for everyone to not feel afraid and to speak up."

I grabbed the sheet music and stood by the microphone. "Can we start practicing it now? I'm dying to learn it! And I have a feeling I'm going to need to be singing this to myself all week. . . ."

After I left my Wildflowers practice, I felt invigorated, better than I had in days. My band knew me and saw me for who I was—and they appreciated me! Maybe if I spoke up to Claire and others, it would go just as well.

I was feeling so great that I decided to knock on Isa's door and clear up the whole Twin Day fiasco before it got worse. But when I knocked, I was met with her usual churlish response.

"What *is* it?" she called, as if people had been pounding on her door all afternoon.

I opened the door and walked in hesitantly. Isa was at her desk studying and chewing on a pencil.

"Sorry to bother you," I said. "I just want to talk to you about Spirit Week."

"Ah," she said, leaning back in her chair, looking as smug as the Cheshire cat. "Here it is. You're going to try to talk me out of dressing up with you for

Twin Day because you *really* want to dress up with your best-best-bestie, Tamiko, just like last year, even though you would never admit it."

Flustered, I took a step back. Isa knew me so well. Why had I thought she wouldn't guess? We still had our old twin-tuition sometimes.

I wanted to just give up and leave. But then I ran through the lines from Tessa's song in my head, and they gave me courage.

It was time to stand up, speak up.

"No," I said. "Well, not exactly. I wanted to ask you how you truly feel about dressing up for Twin Day. Because you *are* my twin, and you're my only sibling, and *you're* my priority. And before you ask— honestly, yes, I would prefer to dress up with Tamiko because it was so fun last year, but not if it would hurt your feelings in any way."

Instead of looking hurt, Isa looked surprised. Her eyebrows shot way up, and then she grinned. "Wow! You actually just told me the truth about how you feel. Way to go, Sisi."

I took a mock bow, but inside I really was feeling pretty proud. I had said exactly what I meant, politely and kindly, and Isa had listened.

"So really, how do you feel about it?" I asked. "Do you want to dress up with me? Because I'll do it. Team P forever."

Isa grunted. "Please. I'm a twin every day of my life. Why would I want to dress up as one for a school spirit day? I'm not planning to dress up at all during Spirit Week."

Now it was my turn to grin. Isa was Isa, and I loved her for that. Mostly she was spice—grumpy, moody spice—but I knew there was sweetness inside her too, even if she didn't always want to show it.

Maybe we were all Chocolate Chili ice cream.

"Okay," I said, hugely relieved to be able to tell Tamiko we were on for dressing up together. It still didn't solve the problem of Allie feeling left out or me not quitting student council, but hey, I was making progress.

One thing at a time.

I turned to leave Isa's room. But before I did, I leaned back through her doorway and said, "Hey, do you want to dress alike for dinner tonight just to mess with Mami and Papi?"

Isa laughed her big loud laugh, the one I didn't hear too often. She raised her hand to give me an air fist bump. "Great idea, but not tonight. Thanks for asking, though, Sunshine."

It was good to know Isa still thought of me as Sunshine. Maybe I really could tackle this problem. Maybe I could even manage to have fun during Spirit Week.

Stand up, speak up—that was my new motto. All thanks to Tessa.

CHAPTER TWELVE
STAND UP, SPEAK UP

I was sitting at lunch with Tamiko the next day. MacKenzie was in the library studying for a quiz, so Tamiko had spent the previous ten minutes pumping me up to finally, *finally* quit. She'd used a lot of baseball references that I didn't fully understand. But now it was the moment of truth. I knew that if I didn't get up the courage to do it right that very second, it might never happen.

I took a deep breath.

"I'm doing it now," I told Tamiko. "For real. So think good thoughts."

"Should I take a picture of this moment to post on social media? Caption: 'Seventh-Grade Girl Finds Strength She Never Knew She Had'?"

I shook my head. "Tamiko! No. Just—sit tight. I'll be back."

And with that, I marched over to the table where Claire and Vikram were sitting. I hadn't known they were friends outside of student council, but they looked sort of . . . dreamy. I didn't want to intrude on anything, but it was now or never!

"Hi, guys," I said fake-breezily.

"Sierra! Sit down and join us." Claire motioned toward the empty seat beside Vikram.

I wanted to yell to Tamiko, "See? She really is nice sometimes!" But then I reminded myself that we all have sweetness and spice in us. We all do. None of us are just one or the other.

"Thanks, Claire, but I can't stay. I just wanted to let you know . . . that I have to resign from student council. I'm very sorry."

Claire and Vikram looked utterly confused. They exchanged a glance, shoulders raised, palms up, looking like cartoon characters who were saying, "I don't know! Beats me!"

"Sierra!" Claire exclaimed. "*Why?* We love you so much! Why would you leave us?"

My heart felt briefly warmed at how genuinely

Claire had said she loved me. It really was so nice to be liked and even loved. I couldn't help it. But then I remembered Tamiko sitting at the table, waiting for me, and how I hadn't stood up for Allie. I couldn't let compliments and flattery turn me into a person I didn't like.

"I don't think it's a good fit for me," I said diplomatically, mentally thanking Mrs. Leone for her advice.

"Why?" asked Vikram. "You're a great secretary. Your handwriting is so neat."

"Yes!" agreed Claire. "We really need you. Stay for the rest of the year, okay? Please?"

I could see I'd have to really lay it on the line here and be totally and completely honest, the way I'd been with Isa. I was going to have to go whole hog, Chocolate Chili–flavored Sierra.

"I'm sorry, but I can't stay on the council. And I really think you guys should get rid of Anti–Vista Green Day."

Claire bristled visibly. "Why would we do that? Anyway, we can't. We already voted on it and publicized it. *You* made the posters, remember?"

Chocolate Chili, I chanted in my mind. *Stand up,*

speak up! Say what's on your mind! It's time for girls to stop being just kind!

I probably looked like a wacko, standing there, silently running song lyrics through my head, but I didn't care.

I inhaled and exhaled deeply. Then I said, "Yes, I did make the posters, and I'm mad at myself for doing that. It's a hateful theme, and I think it reflects badly on MLK and on the student council to go through with it. Vista Green isn't the enemy. They're another school, just like ours. This isn't like a fun pep rally thing. It's genuinely mean-spirited. And I can't participate in that. Especially since one of my best friends goes there."

Vikram and Claire were quiet for a moment. Then Vikram said, "Well, thanks for telling us, Sierra. You're a quitter, but at least you're honest."

"Yes, *very*," said Claire, looking annoyed.

I knew I didn't have much time left before I'd collapse into a puddle on the floor, but I used my final seconds of bravery to add, "I hope you guys will consider switching to a more fun and inclusive theme, like Throwback Thursday or something. Good luck with Spirit Week."

And I turned and marched back to my table, where Tamiko was waiting, looking as anxious as a mother watching her toddler go down the big slide at the playground.

"Did you do it?" Tamiko squeaked.

I nodded. "I did. I might faint right now, but I did it. And I feel good!"

Tamiko burst into applause, and I prayed that Claire and Vikram wouldn't look over and see us. The conversation hadn't ended too well, and Claire definitely wasn't happy with me, but I'd said what I honestly felt. I'd been polite, I'd been matter-of-fact, and I was on the side of kindness. That had to count for something.

In fact, now that I had actually done it, I could see that speaking up and being sweet could actually go together quite nicely—with a big helping heap of courage. It was almost like one of Tamiko's special ice cream recipes: some courage, some sweetness, and, of course, a sprinkle of happy on top.

Tamiko got up and came around the table to give me a huge hug, right in front of the whole cafeteria. They probably all thought I'd failed a test or something. But I needed that hug right then, and I appreciated it.

"Thanks, Tamiko. You're the *best* best friend."

Saying that reminded me of my final problem—Twin Day, and our *other* best friend, Allie.

"What are we going to do about Allie and Twin Day?" I asked. "She looked like she felt left out when we talked about it on Sunday."

Tamiko thought for a second. Then she said, "Well, why can't she just dress to match us? We'll send her a picture of us, and she can send one of her, and I'll post them all over social media so that to the world, we're all dressed up together for Twin Day."

"That's a great idea! Why didn't I think of that? I'll text her right now and see what she thinks." I whipped out my phone and sent Allie the message, since I knew it was also her lunch period and she was allowed to check her phone.

She wrote back within seconds. Love it! Sprinkle Sundays sisters. Thanks for thinking of me. Then, after a pause, she texted, Any other news?

I knew exactly what she was asking. I proudly texted back, Yep—I did it. Meet your new friend, sweet Sierra, now with a little more spice.

I'm sure I'll love her just as much as the old Sierra, Allied replied. Gotta go. I have a quiz. Talk later!

Tamiko and I spent the rest of the lunch period happily discussing options for our "Triplet" Day outfits. I wanted bright and colorful; Tamiko wanted handcrafted and edgy. We'd have to loop Allie in later for her opinion.

It looked like Spirit Week wasn't going to be so bad after all.

CHAPTER THIRTEEN
SPIRIT WEEK!

After resigning from student council and resolving the Twin Day situation, I felt like an enormous weight had been lifted from my shoulders. I was able to study harder, sing better, focus on tests, and enjoy my dad's Cuban cooking more than ever.

I went to Isa's soccer team finals, and when her team won, my parents took the whole family out for ice cream to celebrate. I was so proud of my sister, and I no longer had any guilt about the upcoming Twin Day. I was able to just be a good sister and help her feel special on such a momentous occasion. And I think Isa appreciated it.

It was great.

I practiced with the Wildflowers twice a week,

and we worked hard on Tessa's new song, until all of us knew our parts perfectly. Every time I sang it, I felt the words with my whole body. It had become my favorite song to perform, and I found myself humming it in the shower, when running drills in soccer, and even in class sometimes, which probably wasn't so great for everyone sitting around me.

Time flew by, and before I knew it, it was finally Spirit Week.

In fact, it seemed that most kids at school wanted Spirit Week to be a positive event, because about a week after I resigned from student council, I noticed that new posters had been put up all over school. They changed Anti–Vista Green Day to Superhero Day and rearranged the schedule.

I didn't know if it was because of what I had said to Claire and Vikram, or if the school administration had made them change it, or if a bunch of students had talked to the student council, or what. But I hoped, and I chose to believe, that it was at least partially because I had stood up and said something.

I was really happy to dress as a superhero. I went as Supergirl. And I hoped that the large *S* on my chest now stood for "Spicy" as well as "Sweet."

While sitting at lunch in my Supergirl costume with Tamiko and MacKenzie, I saw the student council heading our way. They were all in a line carrying their lunch bags, as if they were en route to a table for a lunchtime meeting together. I wondered for a second if I would feel bad that I wasn't included anymore, but I didn't. I felt glad to be where I was.

"Hi!" I said as they passed by. "Great costumes."

I braced myself for Claire or Lee or someone to sneer at me, or just ignore me altogether. But they didn't. They all waved at me, including Claire, and didn't look particularly angry or upset.

Hanna was last in line and lingered after the others had passed. When they were out of earshot, she leaned over our table and said, "Thanks for speaking up about Anti–Vista Green Day, Sierra. I agreed with you that it was a bad idea. I was just too scared to say anything."

"I understand," I said. "I'm really glad it all worked out. Superhero Day is so much fun!"

Hanna nodded. "I'm sad you're not on the council anymore, though. It was nice seeing you every week. You're really kind, and I'll miss you. I'll have to stop by Molly's again and visit when you're working!"

I was touched by Hanna's words—especially the word "kind." I liked being called "kind" much better than "sweet." Being sweet just meant being pleasant, but kindness meant thinking of others.

"I'm going to miss seeing you too," I said to Hanna. "I hope you'll come to Molly's a lot!"

"I will," Hanna said. "It's the best ice cream in town." She smiled and hurried off to join the rest of the student council, who had sat down at a table in the back. Hanna hurriedly pulled out the familiar green notebook that I had carried around for so long. It looked like Hanna had stepped into the role of secretary in my absence.

"All's well that ends well," said Tamiko, breaking my train of thought.

"You sound like my mom!" I told her.

"Mine too," said Tamiko. "Where do you think I heard it?"

We both laughed, and I finished up my sad-looking cafeteria lunch. It was surprisingly filling, but it still left me hungry for something else . . . something a little spicy and a little sweet.

"You know what I could go for right now?" I asked Tamiko. "Some of Molly's Chocolate Chili ice cream."

Tamiko, who was doing something on her phone, looked surprised. "Seriously? But you don't even like Chocolate Chili ice cream!"

"What makes you say that?"

Tamiko rolled her eyes and laughed. "Sierra— you have *no* poker face. When you first tasted it, you looked like you'd accidentally eaten a bug."

I was horrified. Was I really that obvious? "Did Mrs. Shear notice?"

Tamiko giggled. "Probably. We all did. But you said you liked it, and Allie and I genuinely liked it. So it didn't really matter."

"I didn't like it at first," I admitted. "But then it grew on me. And now I've decided I need a little spice in my life! And anyway, not everyone needs to like every single flavor, right? That's why Molly's sells a variety."

The next day was Twin Day. Tamiko and I planned to meet in the girls' bathroom in the math hall before school to check each other's outfits, which, at long last, we'd agreed on with Allie.

We were all wearing Molly's Ice Cream T-shirts, black jeans with some embroidery around the pockets (done by Tamiko, of course), neon sneakers, and our hair in two messy buns, kind of like a modern Princess Leia. Tamiko and I snapped a picture of ourselves and sent it to Allie, who sent us one of herself in return. We looked perfect!

All day we got compliments on our outfits, and Tamiko made a point to show everyone the picture of Allie as well. Some kids thought it was a little strange that we would celebrate one of our school's Spirit Week dress-up days with someone from another school, but most kids, especially the ones who knew Allie, thought it was really neat. After all, she was showing that she still had love and spirit for MLK!

Vista Green and the kids who went there weren't our enemies. It was just another school!

Then I got an idea. "Hey, I don't have a council meeting or, well, *anything* after school today! How about we meet Allie at Molly's for some ice cream, and we can all see each other dressed up?"

Tamiko's fingers once again flew over her phone's screen as she sent the invite to Allie.

A second later her phone dinged. "We're on," she said. "Save room for dessert." I wanted to see Allie in her twin outfit, of course. But I had another motive for setting up our after-school ice cream date at Molly's.

I had something special I wanted to share with my two best friends. Something I was very proud of.

When Tamiko and I got to Molly's, Allie was waiting for us at a table, already enjoying a cone of Chocolate Chili ice cream.

"Cool outfits," she said with a grin.

"You too," I replied. "Someone very fashionable must have put that together for you."

I went over to the counter and ordered two more Chocolate Chili cones from Tom, one of the college students who worked at Molly's during the week. He was fun and friendly, and he seemed to like working at the ice cream parlor as much as we did. All the customers liked him too.

While standing at the counter, I leaned close and whispered, "Hey, Tom, since there's no one else in here, would it be okay if I played a special song on the speakers? I want my friends to hear it."

"Sure, Sierra. Whatever you want," Tom agreed. He went to scoop the cones, and I set my phone to Molly's Wi-Fi network and cued up the song. I didn't press play yet.

A minute later I delivered Tamiko's cone and sat

down with my own. I hesitated for a second before taking my first taste, hoping I really did like it and that it hadn't been a fluke the previous time.

It was delicious. The new me really did like Chocolate Chili.

Relieved, I pressed play on my phone, and the song started playing through the speakers.

Immediately Tamiko started humming along. "Hey, what's this song? Do you guys know it?"

Allie shook her head. "I've never heard it before. But it's catchy. I like it!"

I didn't respond, even though I was dying to tell them. I wanted them to figure it out themselves.

"Wait—is this *you* singing, Sierra?" asked Allie. Her voice sounded awed.

I nodded, my cheeks pink, and my smile stretching from ear to ear.

"This is YOU?" said Tamiko, and they both fell silent as they listened to the lyrics.

"Some people say that girls should be good,
But I say, what good does that do a girl?
Stand up, speak up, say what's on your mind.
It's time for girls to stop being just kind!

Some people say that girls should be good,
But I say, what good does that do a girl?
Stand up, speak up, to whomever you meet.
It's time for girls to stop being just sweet!"

When it was over, both of my friends burst into applause. Allie clapped so hard, she nearly dropped her ice cream onto the floor. Tom whooped and hollered from behind the counter.

"Way to go, Sierra!" he called.

"That wasn't you on the *radio*, was it?" Allie asked, her eyes wide with disbelief.

I laughed. "Ha! Not yet. Maybe one day. It's a song I recorded with the Wildflowers over the weekend. Tessa wrote the song, and we've been practicing it nonstop for our next gig."

"The song is *perfect*," said Tamiko. "I just love its message!"

I blushed even harder. I was so happy they loved the song as much as I did. "I'm glad, because Tessa wrote it for me! And it has given me so much courage. It has helped me understand that it's okay to be sweet and also have strong opinions and defend them. I will never stand by and let someone insult one of my friends again."

Allie looked at me, and I could see there was almost a tear in her eye. I couldn't believe I'd ever *not* stood up for her. What had I been thinking?

"When will you get to play this amazing song for the public?" Tamiko asked.

"Whenever we get our next gig, I guess. In the meantime, though, let's take a selfie to remember this awesome Twin Day."

We all huddled together, and Tamiko took the picture. Her fingers started moving, and I realized she was preparing to post it. "What should I caption it?" she asked.

Allie and I thought a minute. Then I grinned. I had the perfect caption.

"'Sugar, Spice, and Sprinkles,'" I said. "Because that's the three of us."

"Hey—which one of us is the sprinkles?" joked Tamiko.

I laughed. "All of us. We're all a little bit of everything . . . sweet, spicy, brave, funny. All with a sprinkle of happy on top, of course!"

DON'T MISS BOOK 10:
A SPRINKLE OF FRIENDSHIP

"Okay, Sprinkle Sundays sisters, are you ready?"

My besties, Tamiko and Sierra, each gave a thumbs-up from behind the counter. I switched the sign on the front door from CLOSED to OPEN. "Ta-da! Molly's is open for another beautiful summer day!"

It was a Sunday afternoon, and Tamiko, Sierra, and I were working our usual shift at my mom's ice cream parlor, Molly's.

The bell on the door jingled as our first customers of the day entered the store.

"Let the post-day-camp games begin!" joked Tamiko, while Sierra greeted a mom and two sweaty and tired-looking little boys wearing camp T-shirts.

"Hey, I went to Whalers Camp when I was your age!" said Sierra to the boys, and suddenly they weren't tired at all but were chatting enthusiastically to Sierra about Spikeball tournaments and swim races and skippers-versus-captains team competitions.

Tamiko laughed and shook her head. "I don't know how she does it!"

"What?" I asked, though I was pretty sure I knew what she meant.

"Sierra charms everyone! That girl can't go five minutes without making a new friend!"

I watched as Sierra gave the boys their ice creams and then showed off a complicated Whalers Camp high-five handshake that left them all laughing. "Yeah," I said. "She's living proof of that saying 'A stranger is just a friend you haven't met yet.' I can't relate! I'd pretty much always rather be reading a book instead."

"I agree. Who wants to waste energy on people you don't even know, who might be annoying anyway?"

"Tamiko!" I had to smile because she was so outrageous sometimes. "That's not nice!"

Tamiko shrugged. "I just can't pretend to be interested. Anyway, I already have enough friends."

"But, Tamiko, how can you talk about not needing new friends? You've made all those new friends at the Y!"

With school out for the past month, each of us had done different things. I had gone back up to my old camp, Holly Oaks in New Hampshire, for three awesome weeks of cool weather, arts and crafts, and swimming in the crystal clear lake. I had a bunch of old friends there from when I was little, and I just relaxed and didn't have to worry about my social life. Unlike here at home, where I'd had to move and leave my besties, Tamiko and Sierra, at my old school without me (*and* I'd had to try to make friends at my new school) . . . all because of my parents' divorce.

For the previous five years, I'd gone for the whole summer, and I'd adored it. This year, our budget had only allowed for a half session at Holly Oaks camp. But as consolation, my parents had let me sign up for a food-writing class for kids at the Y here in Bayville, which started tomorrow. I loved reading and writing and food, so I was excited to combine all three in one class, even though I was nervous about meeting all new kids again. Despite what Tamiko had said, she was actually pretty good in the friend-making department, while I was shy.

"Blah, blah, blah," said Tamiko. "That doesn't count. Those kids and I share interests, like colleagues, so it's more like networking. We're all artistic and creative, and we all have blogs and portfolios that we help one another with. We have a lot in common. I don't just bond with random strangers all over the place, like this one!" She jerked her thumb at Sierra, who had sent the happy customers on their way and joined our conversation.

"What? I'm not bonding with random strangers! Those kids go to my camp!"

Tamiko and I looked at each other, and we both rolled our eyes. "I give up," she said. "You could find common ground with anyone, Sierra. Look at all the new friends you've made this year! No rhyme or reason."

Sierra bristled. "That's not true! MacKenzie is in my science class. The girls from my band are . . . in my band. The student council kids . . . well, forget about them. The kids from soccer and softball—we have our teams in common."

"Right, but what about Jenna, who you met at the park; and Sweeney, your 'cat-sitting' friend; and Philip from the pet food store?"

Sierra just shrugged and shook her head. "What can I say? I'm a people person!"

"And don't forget all her rock-band camp friends!" I added quietly.

Sierra and the rest of her band, the Wildflowers, had attended a local rock-band camp this summer. Since I'd been back for a week, I'd noticed that all the kids from the program had been stopping by the store and trying out songs for one another. My mom had even let Sierra play Wildflowers songs on the store's sound system once she'd approved it. Molly's Ice Cream was suddenly getting a reputation as a talent incubator for local bands, and I wasn't quite sure I liked it. I had wanted the store to be more of a literary ice cream parlor, and had even introduced a few bookish traditions early on, like book and ice cream pairings, that had kind of fallen by the wayside.

"Oh, well, the Wildflowers are such a great group of people, and we have so much fun at our weekly jam sessions. I always learn something new from each of them. For example, Reagan just did a Kickstarter campaign—"

Tamiko did a facepalm and shook her head. "I'm so sorry I have to leave you to deal with this crazy socialite by yourself while I'm away, Alley Cat!"

Sierra just grinned and shook her head at us.

Tamiko and her family were leaving the next day for their vacation in Japan. I was dreading her departure, since she was so much fun and the three of us were so well balanced as a work team and best-friend group. It was funny, but I almost felt nervous about it being just Sierra and me alone. Tamiko had a way of speaking the truth, clearing the air, and calling us on any silliness, and she always kept everything running smoothly.

Plus, I didn't have a ton of friends, so with Tamiko away, 50 percent of my best friends would be gone.

I guessed Sierra felt sad about it too, because she moaned, "It's not going to be the same without you here, Tamiko!"

Tamiko sighed dramatically. "I'm going to Japan, not another planet," she said. "And it's only for three weeks. We'll keep in touch via SuperSnap, and we can even FacePage if you want. Instead of being sad, think of all the cool souvenirs I'm going to bring you back from Tokyo. You know, in Japan it's a tradition for businesspeople to bring souvenirs—usually food—back for their coworkers when they go on business trips."

My mom had just come into the front of the store from her office. She heard us chatting and said, "And all the ice cream research you're going to do for me makes this kind of like a business trip!"

"Mmm! I can't wait!" said Tamiko, patting her stomach.

My mother had given Tamiko fifty dollars to spend on researching the "soft cream" flavors in Japan. Soft cream was like our soft-serve ice cream—and it was popular for its unusual regional flavors, like soy sauce or yam or corn. Since my mom was always looking for new ideas to keep things at Molly's exciting, and since Tamiko was such a good trend-spotter, we had high hopes for Tamiko's post-trip recommendations.

"We can't wait to hear what you find. Check in often and hurry back!" I said wistfully.

"We're all going to miss you, Tamiko, but hopefully we won't have much time to be sad," my mom said.

We all looked at her, confused.

"It's summer! Ice cream season!" she reminded us. "We'll be so busy, the time will go by like that." She snapped her fingers for emphasis.

I nodded. "That's true. Hopefully we'll blink, and—presto!—Tamiko will be back."

Tamiko made a fake-annoyed face. "Well, you can miss me *a little*," she said, and everyone laughed.

Then the post-lunch crowd started to roll in and we got busy.

Besides a steady stream of day campers, a number of Sierra's music friends came in, including one of her bandmates, Tessa, who made me a little nervous. She had a crush on my good friend Colin from my new school, and . . . so did I, I guess. I made myself busy with another kind of crush while Tessa was there— crushing toppings at the back counter (okay, hiding) while Sierra chatted with her.

I caught the name "Colin," and my ears perked up.

". . . haven't seen him much at all," Sierra was saying.

My blood boiled a little bit. It was true that he hadn't visited Molly's since I'd returned from camp, but I didn't want Tessa to know that.

"Me neither," Tessa said.

Well, that was good anyway. If I wasn't seeing him, at least *she* wasn't either.

Sierra and Tessa chatted about new lyrics for a song they were both struggling to finish. I heard the bell jingle, and a bunch of Tamiko's photography "friends" (colleagues?) came in. I sighed and let her handle their orders while I cleaned and prepped. If things got crazy—which they would, shortly—I'd rejoin the fray and take orders. For now, I preferred to stay in the background and feel sorry for myself about not having a lot of friends who could visit me at work.

After a little while, Tamiko called, "Allie! Rush! All hands on deck!"

I washed up and joined the girls at the counter. There was a line almost out the door, and I'd been so lost in my own world that I hadn't even noticed!

By the time things settled down, almost an hour and a half had passed. We'd been so busy, I hadn't even had time to look at the clock. *Gosh,* I thought. How were Sierra and I going to handle these crowds when it was just the two of us? Maybe things really *would* be so crazy with Tamiko gone that the time would fly.

Later, as we cleaned up the mess we'd made during

the rush, Sierra began singing her new Wildflowers song. It was all about loving someone she hadn't met yet.

I couldn't help but laugh. "Sierra, you are so funny! You love meeting people so much that your songs are about loving people you haven't even met yet!"

"Well, hey, it's true! All our future boyfriends are out there somewhere right now!"

Tamiko folded her hands and put them to her cheek in a fake-dreamy pose. "Yes, and mine's so busy inventing a new social media app that will take the world by storm, he has no time to meet anyone else."

We all chuckled, and Sierra said, "Well, my future boyfriend is busy writing incredible songs that the whole world will sing along to one day!"

I kept wiping the counter, but I was smiling.

"How about you, Allie?" joked Sierra. "What's Colin up to right now?"

I swiped at her with the rag, and she jumped away, shrieking.

"I don't even know where Colin is these days!" I said, trying to keep my voice light.

"Wait. Haven't you texted him since you got back from camp?" asked Tamiko.

I shrugged.

"Why not?" asked Sierra. "The last time I saw him, he asked me when you'd be back."

"He did?" I tried to hide my smile.

Sierra nodded. "Maybe he doesn't know you're home."

"Allie, he's, like, your best friend at Vista Green. Why haven't you told him you're back?" said Tamiko. "That's weird."

"I . . . I just didn't want to seem like I was stalking him."

"You weirdo! How would it be stalking to tell a close friend that you're home after being away for a long time?"

I shrugged again.

"Were you hoping his love radar would make him magically sense you were back and he'd just appear?" Tamiko teased.

I swatted her with the rag, but she wasn't completely wrong. I had told Colin more or less when I'd be coming home, and I had hoped he'd be keeping track and contact me as soon as I'd returned. But he hadn't.

"Maybe *he's* worried about acting like a stalker,"

said Sierra thoughtfully. She was so kind that she always looked at every side of a situation.

I hadn't really thought of it that way, but I pushed that idea out of my mind. I still wanted *him* to come find *me*! "Maybe," I said.

Tamiko and Sierra exchanged a glance. "Don't be a shy little turtle," said Tamiko. "You have to stick your neck out sometimes."

Sierra pushed her head forward like a turtle to illustrate, and we all gigged.

It was all well and good for Sierra to stick her neck out, but I *was* a shy little turtle. I'd do anything to avoid sticking my neck out. Even if that meant not texting a so-called crush.

I checked my SuperSnap account one last time before I powered down my phone. Colin wasn't the best social media user even during the school year, but I'd hoped he would at least post a few photos so I could see where he was. Like, was he even *in* Bayville right now? And if so, where was he?

I sighed and then took a deep breath in for courage, like my dad had taught me. I was outside my new classroom at the Y, and was ready to learn all about food writing for three hours a day, two mornings a week. What I *wasn't* ready for was a sea of new faces.

I gripped the doorknob and pushed with a sweaty palm. The door didn't open. I could see kids sitting inside and the teacher at the desk. It didn't look like they had started yet, but it was one minute before start time. I pushed again. Was the door locked? I gave the doorknob a rattle, and a bunch of people looked up at the door. My face started a slow burn from the bottom up; the feeling of the heat rising in my cheeks made me even more embarrassed, so I blushed harder. I'm sure my face was scarlet. I gave the door one more yank, and in doing so, I also somehow pulled it, and the door opened.

Pull, not push. Good one, Allie.

I stumbled into the classroom awkwardly, and a few of the kids giggled. Not meanly, but it was still embarrassing that they had noticed me at all.

"Good morning!" said the teacher cheerfully.

I mumbled a good morning and headed to the last row of the classroom. Just as I set my bag down on the desk, the teacher called, "We're not too big a group, so let's all try to stay toward the front of the room, please. It makes for better conversation, okay?"

Everyone swiveled to look at me. I nodded and trudged back toward the front of the room, and selected a seat behind a very large boy who would hide me well.

Phew. Safe.

I settled into my seat and darted a few glances around at the other kids. From what I could see, there were around sixteen of us, equally split between boys and girls, some a little older than I was, but not super-old. Probably early high school, like ninth graders.

"All right. I think it's time we get started!" said the teacher, standing up at the front of the classroom. "I'm Valerie Gallo, and I'm super-excited to be your instructor for this course. I love cooking and food, and talking and writing about cooking and food, and I am really looking forward to getting to know you all. I think we'll cook up some great things in this course together, haha!"

Everyone chuckled politely, and Ms. Gallo grinned.

I recognized her name from her byline in our local paper, the *Daily Chronicle*. She was one of the two food writers on staff there, and she often reviewed local restaurants. Her food descriptions always made my mouth water. I was psyched that I was going to hear her instructions on food writing.

Ms. Gallo had us go around the room and intro-duce ourselves. Because I was in the back, I went last, and by the time they got to me, I was in a state of total panic at having to speak. The other kids had said their names, grades, and schools, and then had given some detail about their passions for food and/or writing. I just wanted to get it over with, so I didn't plan to go into much detail.

"I . . . uh . . . I'm Allie Shear. I'll be an eighth grader at Vista Green . . . and I love food!" I babbled nervously.

"Welcome, Allie!" said Ms. Gallo with a warm smile. "Well, let's get started. Is anyone here familiar with M.J. Connor's work?"

Of course! I thought excitedly. She was one of my favorite writers of all time. My school librarian, Mrs. K., had given me one of her books to read this year. M. J. Connor was one of the most acclaimed food writers ever. I adored her work.

I was nodding at Ms. Gallo, but when I looked around and realized that no one else was, I quickly stilled my bobbing head. The last thing I wanted was for the teacher to notice and call on me to explain anything about Connor and her work in front of all these other kids. Luckily, the boy in front of me—Sam—had hidden my nodding head from her view.

"Okay. Well, then let me tell you about her and

her glorious food writing," said Ms. Gallo. "One of my favorite things about her work is her choice of words. Certainly, all writing comes down to word choice." She laughed a little. "But let's think about how in food writing, just the right word can make all the difference between good and bad. Think of 'crisp green lettuce' and 'limp green lettuce.' A big difference, right? Or look at peanut butter—chunky or smooth? It's all in the choice of words. . . . Try to keep from being too *ordinary*, as blandness is the kiss of death in writing *and* in cooking. . . ."

And we were off and running, and I was in heaven.

Ever since Molly's had been interviewed for articles in the local paper and for a gourmet food website, I'd been into food writing. I wrote a column for my school newspaper called Get the Scoop, where I reviewed books and then suggested an ice cream treat to pair with the book while the person was reading it. The column had been popular, and Colin had even told me once that his older sister (who was in high school) read it religiously. Crazy!

Between brainstorming flavors with my mom, watching Tamiko concoct wild parfaits and promotional ice cream sundaes, and reading food writing in magazines and books suggested by Mrs. K., I'd had a pretty foodie year. Plus, Tamiko and Sierra and I adored going to the food truck park at our local mall and trying new dishes all the time. I loved the fact that good food writing inspired all of my senses—I could picture the food and imagine the smell and taste, as well as the texture in my mouth. The best food writing made me instantly hungry and excited, and it was a skill I'd love to develop. Maybe someday I could have a job like Ms. Gallo's, and combine food and writing for a living. That would be so ideal.

Now Ms. Gallo was up at the SMART Board, asking us for descriptive words that would be good for food writing. Kids were calling out as she scribbled in green marker.

"Crispy!"

"Juicy!"

"Thick!"

I had so many words that I could call out, but I was too shy.

"Let's hear from the back row," said Ms. Gallo, as if reading my mind.

I thought of M. J. Connor and one of my favorite excerpts from her description of a meal in France.

"Cushioned," I croaked in a voice rusty from disuse.

"Yes!" cried Ms. Gallo. "Who said that?"

Tentatively I raised my hand.

"Um, Allie?"

I nodded.

"Have you read M. J. Connor?"

I nodded again.

Ms. Gallo grinned. "Great. Are you thinking of 'Cushions of toast softened with creamy pats of sweet butter'?"

I grinned back and nodded yet again.

"Nice," said Ms. Gallo, a glint of admiration in her eye. "Who else?" she asked as she looked around the room.

This always happened to me: I always befriended the teacher. Somehow it was safer than dealing directly with the other kids, and it created a little bubble for me so that I didn't really need to interact with anyone else.

The morning went on with us collecting words and copying them down, and Ms. Gallo quoting her favorite writers and recommending books for us to read. It was kind of freewheeling, though she said that once we had each written a piece to work with, probably by the next class, we'd split up into more of a workshop setting, with kids in small groups or partnerships for half of each class. Ugh. *Awk*-ward! I was not looking forward to *that*.

"Your assignment!" Ms. Gallo announced as the clock struck noon. "Write a review of an exciting restaurant. Bonus points if you go and actually have a meal there between now and Thursday's class! I want five hundred words. No groans! You can do it. Remember to account for ambiance and service as well as the food. Thanks for coming today, and good luck! *Bon appétit!*"

I quickly packed my things and rushed out. I was due to work at Molly's at one o'clock, and the bus ride would take twenty minutes at least. That's what I told myself, anyway. It was more that I really didn't want to have to chat with anyone.

As I speed-walked out of the building and down the block to the bus stop, my heart raced with a feeling of exhilaration. I was thrilled by the teacher and the class, but I was even more thrilled that I'd escaped without having to interact with any of the kids. What a relief to not have to do the whole awkward getting-to-know-you conversation with any randoms (to use Tamiko's word). Maybe I could partner with the teacher for the workshop in the next class. It would be oh-so-much easier.

On the bus I powered up my phone and checked Colin's SuperSnap again. Nothing. My fingers hovered over the screen as I debated whether or not to text him. I had his contact info right there in the palm of my hand, and I missed him. Would it be so awful if I sent a breezy little text? What about something like, "Hey, Colin. Hope your summer is great so far! Stop by for an ice cream at Molly's on the house so I can hear all about it!" But was the free ice cream part desperate? Like, was I bribing him to come see me? And if I didn't say "on the house," was I basically asking him to come and spend money to see me? But how else could I phrase it? Ugh. Totally befuddled, I locked the phone, dropped it back into my bag, and stared out the window. I thought about asking Tamiko for advice, but then I realized she was on the plane, flying across the Pacific Ocean. I missed her already.

Monday afternoons at Molly's were pretty quiet, it turned out, even in the summer. Probably because so many people got ice cream on the weekends and Mondays were all business for them, but it made for a slow afternoon.

Sierra and I were both working, but there really wasn't enough for us to do. The topping jars and bins were all full, the counters and floor sparkling, the bathroom shining, and the ice cream freezer bursting with fresh bins of cool ice cream flavors. Even the few customers seemed a little uninspired on a Monday. One lady ordered a vanilla shake. A plain vanilla shake! Tamiko never would have stood for an order like that if she were there. She would have encouraged the woman to think outside the box and order something great, or convinced her to let Tamiko surprise her with a creation. But without Tamiko there, Sierra and I just smiled and made the shake and rang up the lady's order. Ho hum.

In between helping customers, Sierra sang some new songs she'd written, to test them out on me and get my reaction.

"I'm just a lonely girl. Are you lonely too? Maybe I'm the girl for you," Sierra sang out. "And then I'll point to the audience. What do you think?"

"It's okay," I said slowly.

"Just okay?" Sierra looked at me seriously. "Come on. You're holding back. What don't you like about it?"

"No, no, no, I don't mean I don't like it," I said. "It's just . . . a little . . ." I searched for the right word, thinking of Ms. Gallo and her focus on word choice. "Ordinary?"

Sierra looked confused. "I don't understand."

I sighed. "'Lonely *too*. I'm the girl for *you*.' What's the next verse? 'Without you I'll go *boo-hoo*'?"

Thankfully, Sierra didn't get insulted; she just laughed. "I'm sorry," I said. "It's just that some of the other songs you sing have such meaningful words. I know pop music is supposed to be light, but I just think you can do a little more with this one."

Sierra nodded in agreement. "Maybe it's because there's not a special person in my life to think about while I sing it," Sierra said. "You know, the way Tamiko has Ewan, and you"—Sierra paused for dramatic effect, and her eyes sparkled—"have Colllllllin." She sang his name out.

I blushed. "I don't 'have' Colin," I said. "He's just a friend. A friend I . . . maybe kinda sorta like. A little bit."

"Well, that's still more than I have," Sierra said.

"All I have is my cat." She sang loudly to no one in particular, "Where are youuuuuu, my little pet? I'm missing you, and we haven't even met!" Sierra turned to me with a grin. "Hey, that's pretty good. I'm gonna write that down so I don't *forget*. Haha!"

The two customers who were sitting at a table clapped. Sierra took a silly bow. "I'll be signing autographs before you leave!" she joked, and they smiled and nodded. "See?" she said to me. "I knew it was good!"

I rolled my eyes, but I had to smile, too. *Even when she's just fooling around, Sierra finds a way to connect with people,* I marveled. I could barely even speak in a room full of people who shared my interests, never mind break out into song in front of total strangers.

I thought of school this past year and how long it had taken me to speak up, even with great encouragement from, say, my favorite teacher—Ms. Healy. She'd worked so hard to get me to talk in English class, enticing me with little tidbits that she knew about me from conversations we'd had outside of class; bringing up my favorite book, *Anne of Green Gables*; asking me point-blank questions I couldn't squirm away from.

It had finally worked. By the end of the year I'd been able to speak out loud in her class every day.

I also thought about the school librarian, Mrs. K., and how she'd drawn me out with all of her little kindnesses—taking me to the Book Fest at my old school and giving me great things to read. (Hello, M. J. Connor!)

Colin, too, had made an effort with me, inviting me to sit with him on the school bus, saving me from the girls we called the Mean Team, and asking me to write for the school paper. We were actual friends. He was the first friend I'd really made on my own, since my mom had basically picked Sierra and Tamiko for me when we were toddlers—so Colin being the first friend I had chosen myself was kind of significant.

I didn't have a ton of other friends at school, and I generally kept to myself. If I disappeared from Vista Green, I wasn't sure too many people would notice, beyond Colin and those two teachers. Maybe also Amanda, whose mom lived in my dad's building. We were friends, you could say. I probably would have been hanging with her if she hadn't been at camp for the summer. But I was always relieved to get home at the end of the school day and be alone—to nestle into my window seat at my mom's or into my comfy marshmallow armchair at my dad's. The way I'd felt like I'd escaped from food-writing class, that was kind of how I felt every day when I got home from school.

But now that I'd been away from school for five weeks or so, it all felt like a dream. Had I really switched schools last year? Left my two besties and everything I knew behind? Had I really worked in the library and written for the school paper? Had I really tutored kids at the town library? I guessed I had, but it was hard to imagine doing it all again. I dreaded restarting it all, rekindling the relationships, just as I dreaded having to interact with all new kids in my food-writing class. It would be so much easier to just hide at home with a book!

The two customers stood up to leave, and Sierra looked up from the notebook where she was writing down lyrics. "Good-bye, my darling fans!" she called after them. "I'll be performing every weekday afternoon, from one to six, and Sundays from one to eight. Come on back!"

Looking for another great book?
Find it
IN THE MIDDLE.

Fun, fantastic books for kids
in the in-be**TWEEN** age.

IntheMiddleBooks.com

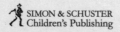